MY AMERICAN BOYFRIEND

This is a work of fiction. Similarities to real people, places, or events are entirely coincidental.

MY AMERICAN BOYFRIEND

First edition. November 4, 2024.

Copyright © 2024 C. S. MacInnes.

ISBN: 979-8991571302

Written by C. S. MacInnes.

To my nieces and nephews.

Never let anyone tell you that you cannot do anything you put your mind to. If you can dream it, you can achieve it.

Love Uncle C

BY
C.S. Mac Innes

Chapter 1
FAMILY

I was sitting in my room, looking out the window as I worked on my schoolwork for my final year before heading off to university. Growing up in the highlands of Scotland, there weren't many opportunities unless you were willing to travel to England, attend a major university, and then land a job out there. For most in my small village, they stayed and ran their family farms. This was what my grandad wanted of me.

My grandad was a traditional man. His father was a sheep farmer, his granddad was a sheep farmer, and so on. As far back as one could remember, our family had been sheep farmers, so much so that if you owned anything made of Scottish wool, it most likely came from my family's farm. Grandad wanted me to take over the farm; he'd been saying since I was a young boy that he would give me control and start his retirement with my grandma once I was eighteen. He'd wanted to leave the business to my mum, but she decided to marry a solicitor instead of the son of a cattle rancher that my grandad wanted her to marry. Mum had wanted to marry for love, and Grandad had wished to expand the business. He hadn't cared about love and still said it wasn't essential; family was, and doing what was best for the family should come first. He reminded me all the time that while he loved my grandma and she loved him, they'd married one another as it was what made sense to improve both families. He kept telling me that when the time came, I should marry a young lady who would make the business and family better and that I would learn to love her as he did Grandma.

Mum was a tall woman with long red hair and a slender figure. She'd wanted a life that she could enjoy, free from the everyday running of a farm and the sheep, so when she met my father at university, she saw her chance to change her life. She and my father dated while in university and after graduation she came back to the village. He followed and opened a practice here. They married a year later, and two years after that, I was born. When Mum decided to help Dad run his practice and not take over the farm, Grandad was less than pleased. A massive fight sent a rift through the family, and they didn't talk until I was born. Having a grandson made Grandad the happiest man alive as he now had an heir to his family's farm and legacy. He told everyone in the village how he was proud that someone wanted to take over his farm and keep the family business alive. He'd had me working on the farm since I was old enough to walk and talk. This didn't please my mother. She always told me, "David, I want you to create your future; I want you to go to university, experience a whole new world, and find a wife and a path that will make you happy. Don't settle for your grandad's choice in life; you aren't him and need to find your own way."

I'd always admired my mother for standing up to Grandad and being her own woman, and deep down, I think Grandma did, too. My grandma was a short, heavy-set woman with a sweet smile that lit up the room when she walked in. She could befriend anyone and would talk to a stranger like she'd known them forever. Grandma spent most of her time in town volunteering for the homeless or those struggling with mental illness. Grandad disapproved of this and felt Grandma should be at the farm taking care of the home while he and the crew were out in the fields and barns, but Grandma still did it anyway. Grandma had always been sweet and loving towards me and told me on many occasions that she wanted me to live my own life but also hoped that I'd take over the farm so that Grandad could be happy and retire. She feared that if I didn't find a lovely wife and take over the farm, Grandad would work until the day he died instead of enjoying the retirement he had so earned. I loved my grandma dearly, but the fact that she wanted me to take over a life that she didn't even want herself always made me feel indifferent to the situation. She wanted me to take over the farm and find a wife who'd help me, yet she tried to spend as much time away from the farm as she didn't want to deal with it or Grandad. I sometimes wondered if that was because Grandad hated my father. Perhaps Grandma was hoping that if I took over the farm, it'd bring the family closer, or maybe she was tired of all the fighting between Mum and Grandad and wanted to get away from this farm, and if that meant making my life into something I didn't want, then so be it. Grandma was not the most educated person and I thought this sometimes clouded her judgment. She didn't seem to understand that sometimes what was easier was not always what was right.

Dad was a tall, handsome man. He came from an Italian family with a fair amount of money and had always wanted a more straightforward, "normal" life. I would never know why he became a solicitor. When he met my mum, he was fascinated by her. Here was this person from a small village in the northern highlands of Scotland who had never seen a large city, who was so full of life and spirit and wanted to create her own path just like him, and he just knew he had to talk to her. When he had the chance, he struck up a conversation, they hit it off, and the rest was history.

When I was born, Dad was thrilled to have a child and made sure I had the best upbringing possible with private tutors and boarding school; he wanted me to have all the advantages in life that he was given as a child, with one significant difference: there was love in our home. His father was a distant man who never showed any affection to his children. I'd never met my father's dad, and he died a few years ago so I never would. Still, from what my father had said, I didn't miss much, though I always wished I was given the chance to meet him and make my own decisions about him. I liked to think he was not much different from Grandad—an older, impossible man who believed his way of life and thinking was the only way.

Dad made sure that Mum and I had the best lives possible. Even though a solicitor was rarely needed in our village, he still did what he had to do to make sure we had everything we needed. He always told me growing up, "Son, when you have a family of your own, you need to be someone who not only follows his dreams but does everything he can to take care of his family." I'd never forgotten this, so when I told Mum and Dad that I was looking at attending university after schooling was done, both of them were thrilled I wanted to continue my education and that I was making my own path. Grandad was less than thrilled, but Grandma convinced him that I was going to university to learn business so I could better manage the farm; this was not my plan, but if it kept a fight from breaking out, then I was fine with letting him think it was.

I'd been accepted into a university in the United States, and when I told Mum and Dad, there were mixed feelings. Mum wasn't sure having me across the world was a wise or safe idea, as I'd never been out of northern Scotland, and my thick accent might make the Americans treat me poorly. Dad was ecstatic; he saw this as my chance to explore and learn more than I ever would from a university close to home and said I would be a fool to pass up such an experience. I agreed with Dad. Still, there was an alternative motive for me wanting to go to a university out of the country and as far away from my family and village as possible. This was that I was gay.

I'd known I wasn't the same as the other boys in my village since I was around ten. All they wanted to do was talk about girls, and as we grew older, when guys would talk about who they were dating or wanted to date, I still never felt any attraction to women. Instead, I was always more interested in my mates and found them more attractive than any girl in our classes. Being from a small conservative village, I hid my thoughts and feelings about other boys, and when asked why I didn't have a girlfriend, I would simply say that I was too busy with school and the farm. This worked out. I'd stuck with this lie for all these years, and no one had been the wiser. I hadn't even told my parents; I didn't think they would have an issue with it, but it would kill my grandad and grandma. I was sure that they were traditionalists, and I didn't want to upset them, so for me, being able to get away and not only learn but also be able to explore who I was was something I'd been looking forward to.

Chapter 2
GRADUATION

The day of graduation arrived, and the village was decorated on every street corner. This made me laugh inside as our village was ancient; it was one of those places you saw in the movies. Brick-paved roads, small cottages with land for farming and livestock, and, if you lived in the central part as I did, old row homes that were 100-plus years old. What made me laugh was that it was decorated like something out of a Hollywood movie, like they were trying to recreate Vegas with all the lights and things. Everyone would turn up and make a day out of it, not like in the States, where everyone had parties after to celebrate. Here it was, one giant party with food and music all over the streets. I was extremely nervous as I was meant to give the graduation speech and was not looking forward to it. I'd always struggled with public speaking. Large crowds made me uncomfortable due to my anxiety and middling depression. Now I was expected to stand in front of around five hundred people and tell all the others graduating that our futures were bright and to expect great things when I knew in my mind most of them were going to stay in the village and never leave as that was just how it was here.

I was sitting in my room looking over my speech, feeling unconfident, when I heard a knock on my bedroom door. "David, are you okay?" It was my mum's voice on the other side.

"I'm fine, just looking over my speech for today," I said, trying to keep my voice from cracking and sounding nervous.

"Okay, dear, your granddad and grandma will be here soon. Don't be too long." With that, I heard her footsteps fading down the hall and the stairs to the main floor. I put my face into my hands and just moaned as I knew that as soon as they got here, they'd all want to know what school I was going to, whether I would be going to the States or staying close. Dad was hoping for the States, while Mum, Grandad, and Grandma all hoped I would stay closer to home for different reasons. I had chosen to go to the States months ago, but I didn't know how to tell them; Mum would cry, and Grandad would be mad as it meant I would not be around the farm for a while to keep learning and eventually take over like he and Grandma wanted. I heard the door open and Mum talking with Grandma and then Grandad's voice. Dad was not home from work, so I started getting ready and headed down the stairs to greet everyone.

When I got downstairs into the living room, Mum was pouring tea while Grandma was chatting about the graduation ceremony later and how exciting it was for me to give the speech. Grandad was sitting in a chair reading his paper with a pipe in his mouth. Grandma looked at me and said in that sweet, calm voice, "Hello darling, how are you doing? We're so excited for you today."

I smiled, leaned over, kissed her cheek, and said, "Good to see you, Grandma. I'm doing fine." Then I approached Grandad and gave him a handshake, as Grandad was not a hugger. From this, he went right into a speech on how it was essential that I stayed close to the family and that he knew I would make the right choice and go to a university close to home and take over the farm this year. The look on Mum's face showed she was not happy with him trying to persuade me into taking over the farm as she wanted me to follow my dreams as she and Dad had.

Grandma could tell that Mum was upset and, wanting to keep the peace, chimed in. "Oh, Harold, darling, the boy has a good head on his shoulders and will do what is right."

This seemed enough to please my grandad; he smiled, flicked his paper to straighten it out, and said, "Good," then returned to reading his article. I looked at Mum, and she gave me the expression of *ignore it, dear*, so I walked into the kitchen to wait for Dad to arrive.

As I entered the kitchen, I saw Dad's car pulling into the driveway and thought, *Oh, thank the lord, now Grandad can bother him instead of me.* It was a bad thing for me to think. Grandad hated my father and they didn't get along, but I didn't need any more stress with having to deal with getting ready for this speech, which I so did not want to do. Dad opened the door and saw the look on my face. "What's wrong?" he asked.

"Grandad is still trying to guilt me into staying close to home and running the farm, and I still haven't decided what I'll do yet." I slid down into the chair at the table, and Dad just looked at me and took a deep breath.

"You know, Mum and I didn't do what our families wanted, and we turned out fine; we have a comfortable life and a son with a great head on his shoulders." He smiled. "Whatever choice you make, Mum and I will support you, but only you can make that choice."

I looked at him and could not help but smile because I knew he was right. I said, "Thanks, Dad, whatever I do, I will make you proud." With that, he smiled, put his hand on my shoulder, and then walked into the living room to greet my grandparents. I just sat there thinking, *How am I going to tell them? What are they going to say? Should I follow my heart and dreams, go to the States, and make my path? Should I please my grandparents and take over the farm?* I moaned as I got up and returned to spend some more time with everyone before I had to prepare for the graduation ceremony.

When I re-entered into the room, it was an odd sight to see my parents and grandparents getting along for once. I didn't want to ruin this moment with my choice of what I would do for university.

"Hello, darling," said my grandma.

Grandad spoke up. "So, what have you decided, son?"

I just stared at them with a pit in my stomach. I did not want to cause a fight right now, not so close to my speech.

Dad chimed in. "Oh, leave the boy alone. He will tell us once he's ready."

Grandad was not pleased with this. "No, we have waited long enough to hear his plan, so what is it, son."

I smiled, doing my best to not let them know that I was freaking out in my mind and trying my very best not to vomit on them. "Well, I haven't decided yet. I hope to make the choice tonight at dinner." I felt confident that this would settle things.

Grandma smiled and said, "Well, that is a more appropriate time to tell us."

Grandad was not having it. He stood up from the chair and said, "Now, Mildred, we have always been soft on the boy as he's our grandson, and knowing his father was not built for farm work, we did our best to make sure he would not make the same mistakes his parents did."

This did not go over well with my dad, and he stood up, and he and Grandad started one of their famous shouting matches. Not wanting to be a part of this, I grabbed my coat, told Mum I would see them at the graduation ceremony, and walked out the door.

As I walked away from the house, hearing the shouting in the distance, I could see the chaos in the streets from everyone getting everything ready for today. I walked over to the stage and looked at the podium. I'd be talking to the entire village in just a few hours. When I started to get a sense of panic again, I heard a female voice come from behind me. "Are you all right, David?"

I turned around to see Samantha, a girl in my grade whom everyone always wanted to see me date. Her father owned a textile company, and Grandad had been trying for years to become their wool supplier; he hoped that Samantha and I would become close and make that happen, and while we were great friends, we never saw each other as more than that. "I'm fine, just thinking about today and how great it's gonna be."

I smiled, and she looked at me and smiled, then said, "Oh, come on, David, we've been friends for years, and I know when something is bothering you."

I thought to myself, *How does she read me so well?* I said, "Fine, you got me. I'm stressed about speaking today, and my family is fighting over what I will do. Should I take over the farm or follow my own path like Mum and Dad?" I sat there blankly, hoping that I made sense and that Samantha could understand what I was going through.

She leaned her head on my shoulder, and we just sat there for some time before she said, "My dad wants me to take over the textile business, and Mum wants me to do something else with my life, but I honestly want to take over the company. I love it. But I know this will make Mum mad. We must do what makes us happy even if it upsets some; we cannot please them all. I know Mum will get over it, and we will be fine, and I'm sure what you decide will make your family happy eventually."

I just smiled as I knew she was right, and we just sat there looking off into the distance.

Now, the time I had been stressing about all day had come. Here we were, all dressed in graduation robes, listening to our guest speaker. I was waiting for my turn to talk, and I could feel my stomach start to knot as though I was going to vomit. As I tried to calm myself, I heard, "Now it's my pleasure to introduce David to come up and give the graduation address to this year's graduating class." I felt sick but stood up, smiled, approached the podium, and gave the best speech of my life. I was charming, confident, and had the crowd going; what I thought would be a complete nightmare turned out as well as one could hope.

When the ceremony was over, I met with Samantha, and we hugged and cheered about being done. She asked me, "So, have you decided on your plan?"

I just looked at her and frowned. "I have, and I'm not sure how I will tell my family, but I've decided to go to the States for university."

Samantha froze. I didn't know if she was shocked that I was leaving or trying to ensure she had heard me correctly. She then said, "Oh...I see. If that's what you want, I support you. You'll go off to university, then come back and take over your grandad's farm." She smiled at this idea of her running her family's textile business and me running the farm.

I looked at her and knew what I was about to say would be devastating to her. "No, actually, I'm not taking over the farm. I want to make my own path in life; I just don't know how I will break it to them."

We both just sat there without a word for what felt like an eternity before Samantha started to speak. "You don't want to stay in the village and run the farm, but I just thought from what I've heard that you were going to take over. I was taking over my family's business so that we could continue to be friends and have families and they could grow together, and now I'm finding out that you're leaving and I'm going to be left here." She started to cry. I knew Samantha never wanted to stay in the village either, but I never thought she was doing it just because she thought I was. Could I have been that blind not to see that she might have had more feelings for me than just friendship? How could I tell her I was gay and needed to get out of here and find the true me?

All of this was a lot to take in while she was still crying, so I had to say something. I looked at her and said, "Well, it's never too late; you can still get out of here, and no matter what, we will always be friends. It doesn't matter if we live in the UK or on the other side of the world; nothing will ever break up our friendship."

This seemed to work in cheering her up. She wiped the tears from her eyes and said, "You're right; it's our lives, and we have to live them for ourselves. Thank you, David, I needed to hear that."

We both laughed and started to walk towards our families, who were sitting and talking to each other. When we got there, Samantha's dad and my grandad were talking about wool and the textile industry while Mum and Grandma were chatting about something from her childhood. Dad and Samantha's mum were both sitting there with the same expression on their faces of *we're hungry, let's eat*. We all said our goodbyes and headed off to our respective dinners.

Chapter 3
DINNER

Dinner was at a lovely restaurant in the center of the village. There was music and laughter all around from the other families who were also celebrating graduation day, but at our table, one could cut the tension with a knife, some of that being because Dad and Grandad were still not talking from the fight they'd had earlier and also because everyone was holding their breath to find out what I was planning on doing. Was I going to take over or was I going to university? I decided to start small and tell them I'd decided to go to university and see how that played out before telling them I wanted to move to the States for it as well.

I cleared my voice to get their attention, and they all looked up and stared. "Well," I said, "I'm sure you all are dying to know what I have decided to do now that I have graduated, and I would like to tell you all that I have made my decision." I could feel their eyes like daggers looking into my soul to try and figure out who would win their debate of what I would do: my parents or my grandparents. I took a drink of water and then went on. "I have decided the best choice is to go to university." Both my parents and grandparents had looks of delight on their faces, and this confused me as I was sure Grandad was going to have a fit.

Grandma was the first to speak. "That's marvelous, dear, we always knew you would choose university first before taking over the farm and business."

My grandad said, "Yes, of course we did; this will make you successful."

I looked at my parents to see if they were going to say anything, but they both gave me the look of *go on, say what else you have to say*. This was it; I had to tell my grandparents I did not want to take over the farm. How would they handle it? Would Grandad storm out? Or would they be happy and understand it might be time to let the farm go? I looked at them and said, "Well, I have decided I don't want to run the farm; I want to find my own path as Mum and Dad did." There it was, out in the open, and there was no taking it back now. I just braced myself for the worst reaction possible.

Grandad frowned as though he was disappointed that I did not want his life, but then said, "I'm aware that the village is not for everyone, and you want to go out and explore the world. Your mum was the same, but she realized her place was here, and one day you will as well." That was all he said, and then he went back to his dinner like nothing had happened. How could this man be so dense not to understand I didn't just want out of running the farm; I wanted out of the village, out of Scotland. I was unhappy here and needed to leave, but I did not want to upset them further so I left it alone.

The remainder of the dinner was uneventful, and we got through it without me making anyone else upset. How wrong I was. At this point, Dad, who had been very quiet all night, finally said, "Wait, you still haven't told us what school you plan on attending." And there it was, now I had to upset Mum at dinner. I was hoping I could tell them in private so that she could act all hysterical and not make a scene in public, but Dad had just ruined that for me.

"Well, I've been giving it much thought, and I've decided that I would like to go to the States to get my education."

I waited for my mum, and it did not take long. "The States?" she said, loud enough that others in the restaurant stopped their conversations to see what was happening. "What do you mean you're going to the States? I told you how this would upset me, and you're going anyway. Is this because your grandparents always push you to take over the farm?"

I looked at her and said, "No, Mum, this has nothing to do with Grandad and Grandma; when Dad and I talked about it the other day, he told me to do what I thought was best for me and that maybe the States would be a good idea."

This set Mum off. She looked at Dad and started screaming, "So this is your fault! You're the one who told him to leave and run off to America. What will he do there? We have no family over there, and he'll be considered different with his red hair and accent. Did you think of that when you were filling his head with ideas of leaving, Franco?" I hadn't heard my mother use my dad's real name in years; they always used pet names, so I knew that he was in trouble.

As calmly as possible, my dad looked at her and said, "Now, dear, look at us. I'm from Italy, and you're from the highlands of Scotland. We met at a university in another country, and we turned out fine. I want David to have the same chance we did when our parents let us leave home and travel to a faraway place to find ourselves. You found yourself in me and made it back home, and I found myself in you and followed you to the end of the earth to make you happy. Now David is being given a chance to do the same thing, and who are we to stop him?"

Grandma chimed in. "But the States are so far away and aren't as safe as the UK was when we let Sylvia go to London for university."

My grandad just chuckled and said, "Not helping, dear."

My dad looked at my mum and said, "You know we have to let him do this, or he will regret it for the rest of his life, and who knows, he might even meet a nice girl over there." Oh god, of course, he would say something like that. If only they knew the truth. Still, I decided now was not the time. Mum was already too upset as it was.

Mum then started to calm down and said, "You're right, we were given a chance, and now we have to let him, but just know I will be going with him to America to make sure he's all set up beforehand."

Dad smiled and said, "We will both go; this will be a fun adventure for our family."

The rest of the dinner was pleasant. Mum and Grandma discussed what I would need for my trip across the pond. Dad and Grandad even had a conversation about how this would be good, and Grandad, being the man he is, even asked who would be paying for it all as he'd only set aside money for me to stay local and run the farm. Everyone was laughing and having a good time, and it was because of me. When we arrived home that night, I felt good that my choice had brought my family closer together, even if it was just for a little while.

I went to my room, pulled out my acceptance letter, and read it.

• • • •

DEAR MR. DAVID RICCI,

We are proud to inform you that you have been accepted to The University of Michigan Ann Arbor this fall semester. Let me be the first to welcome you as a Wolverine.
We look forward to seeing you this fall.
GO BLUE.

• • • •

NOT ONLY WAS I GOING to the States for university, but I was going to one of the best colleges in the country. I felt I would be able to find myself there and be a part of something bigger. I lay on my bed and started to wonder what my life would be like once I got there before drifting off to sleep.

Chapter 4
SCHOOL VISIT

Three weeks had passed since graduation, and telling my family about going to the States for university and planning our visit to Michigan in a few weeks was in full swing. Dad had taken the time off work and booked our plane tickets. Mum and Grandma had been busy ensuring the laundry was done and packed and that we would likely have everything we couldn't find in America packed and ready to go. Dad and I both found this to be silly. Grandad was kind enough to find a nice hotel close to the campus. Even though Mum and Dad kept saying they would take care of it, he would not listen or take no for an answer. Everything seemed to be going perfectly, and everyone seemed to be on board, but I still had a sense of fear and panic in my stomach that would not go away.

There was a knock on the door, and Mum asked me to answer. When I opened the door, there was Samantha with the biggest smile I had ever seen on her face. She pulled me out the door in a flash, saying she needed to talk to me.

"What is it?" I asked her with a low level of fear in my voice.

She was still smiling and said, "I did it."

I just looked at her. "Ummm, did what?" With a confused look on my face.

"I told my dad I don't want to take over the business. I want to go to university and make my own path like you are."

I smiled and hugged her. "Oh my god, I'm so happy for you, and I can't believe you're doing it. Where are you going to university?" I hoped it would be somewhere as fantastic as going to the States.

She frowned and looked down. "Well, Mum and Dad both insist I go to a small university close by, but I want to go to Oxford or somewhere more exciting."

I lifted her chin and told her, "A small university is still better and a great start that could lead you to a larger, more exciting one."

She smiled at this, and we talked for hours on the steps of my house about our plans and when our visits would be. She even asked me if I would accompany her and her parents on the visit to the university she would be attending. It was only a two-hour drive, and I agreed.

That weekend, Samantha, her parents, and I loaded into her father's SUV and started the trip to the university. We arrived, and I looked up to see a charming small school with open fields and old stone buildings, like something out of a fairy tale. Samantha's eyes lit up, and I knew she would be happy here. We spent the day touring the grounds and buildings, meeting current students, and learning the school's history. The more I saw and heard, the more I became excited about my school visit in the following weeks.

That evening, Samantha's dad took us all out to dinner. We had a pleasant conversation about the school and the classes Samantha would be taking in the fall semester, and everything was perfect. This was until Samantha's mum turned to me and said, "Now, David, I hear you're attending the States for university. Is this true?"

I looked at her and smiled. "Why yes, my parents and I are traveling to Michigan in two weeks to check out the university and find me housing there."

Samantha stood up and ran off after hearing me say this. Her parents looked confused before I stood up, excused myself, and went to find her.

I found her sitting in the hallway by the bathroom crying. I approached her and asked, "Sam, what's wrong?"

Still trying to pull herself together, she said, "I still can't believe you're leaving. There's no one else around here I get along with and no one else to talk to, and now I'm losing you."

I hugged her and did my best to comfort her, but then she reached up and kissed me, and I pulled away. This surprised both of us, and she quickly said she was sorry. We headed back to the dinner table and went on like nothing had happened, but I knew we would have to talk about it at some point. But for the moment, we were happy and back to Sam being excited about school.

Once we were back in our village, Samantha walked me home, and before she left, she started to say how sorry she was for the kiss. She was upset, and it was stupid.

I looked at her and said, "I'm sorry I pulled away; it's not you. It's...its...I don't feel that way about any girl."

She looked at me, confused. "What are you saying, David?"

I just sighed and said, "You're my closest friend, and I need you to keep this a secret, but I'm gay and have known for years but have been unable to express it."

She hugged me. "Oh, David, I am so happy you felt confident enough to tell me, and I promise I won't say anything."

I smiled and hugged her back. It felt good to tell someone. We chatted briefly before saying our goodbyes, and I headed inside to prepare for my school visit.

The day had come. We got up early, Grandad drove us to the airport, we said our goodbyes, and off to America, we went. The flight was uneventful; Mum and Dad debated on-campus housing versus off while I reviewed the information about getting classes scheduled and orientations one could join. There seemed to be so much to do in Ann Arbor, and I wanted to experience as much as possible on this trip and hoped it would help Mum feel more confident about me attending school so far away. There were theaters, gardens, and sporting events, with restaurants of all different cuisines from around the world, and I wanted to know about all of them. Mum tried to ensure it was all safe, and Dad was going along for the ride. We collected our luggage and went straight to the hotel when we landed. I was too excited and asked if I could explore, and they both agreed.

I stepped out of the hotel and thought, *Here I am; I have finally reached a place where I can be me.* There were so many sights and sounds, and I did not know where to go first, so I just started walking. I came across many white tents with other students crowding around them. I looked at a few and noticed booths about the different organizations on campus; from the reading I did on the plane, I looked for some of the ones that interested me. I talked with the people working the booth for a while and even looked at others that might fit my personality, but I wanted to know more. I'm more of a nerdy history buff; while I have an athletic build thanks to working on the farm, being a part of sports never interested me.

I saw a tent that said *soccer*. I had heard from a mate back in Scotland that in America, football is called soccer, and football is a whole different sport entirely. It always confused me as to why the Americans had to be so silly and rename the sports like that. But I enjoyed playing football (soccer) and walked up to get more information. The man at the desk was a very tall and muscular guy named Allen; he was as handsome as he was charming. He told me about this being a club program offered by the city and not the university, and honestly, I did not hear anything else. I was mesmerized by him and found him to be the most handsome man ever. His full head of black hair and tan complexion gave him the look of being from a Latin country, plus he was built like someone who spent more time at the gym than needed.

I snapped out of my mesmerized trance to hear him say, "Would you like to join?"

I looked at him and, like an idiot, my answer was, "Do you play?"

He laughed and said, "Yes, I play every chance I get. We do this for fun if that's what you're worried about."

I wasn't worried about it, but I did not want to let this stranger know I was crushing on him hard. I signed up and got all the information I needed. I noticed that I would be back in Scotland when practice started and let him know.

Allen looked at me and said, "That's okay; here's my contact info. Let me know when you're settled, and we'll get you on a team and go from there."

I smiled and walked off. My mind was racing at this point. I'd found a guy I was attracted to, and we had a shared interest, but there was no way he was gay or, even if he were, would be interested in me. I sighed and returned to the hotel where my parents were out cold from the long trip. I lay on my bed and went to sleep.

The next day I spent touring around the University much as I did with Sam and her parents; Mum was in love with it and was starting to relax a bit, but Dad was still trying to find a good place for me to stay while here, as he was still wanting to give me the best like he had done my whole life. We ended up finding a lovely flat that was close to campus and met Dad's high standards and Mum's safety concerns. It came fully furnished so I just had to bring my belongings, so we rented it and started making plans for what I would need to complete it and make it home for the next four years. When leaving the building, Mum was not watching where she was going and almost got knocked over by a big, tall guy. He apologized before looking up and making eye contact with me. It was Allen from the day before. "Hey, David, was it?" he said.

"Yes, that's correct," I responded.

Dad looked at him and shook his hand. "Hello, I'm Franco, David's father, and this is his mum Sylvia. How do you and David know one another?"

I was turning bright red with embarrassment.

"Oh, David and I met yesterday when he signed up to play soccer this fall."

My father looked at me with an expression of pride.

"Well, that's just lovely," my mother said.

"Sure is," said Dad. He then turned towards Allen and asked, "Do you live in this building?"

Allen said, "Why yes, I do. I moved in last semester, and it's a perfect place to live."

Hearing this made Mum very pleased. "Well, that's just fantastic; we just rented a flat for David in this building, and knowing it's a nice place to live and that David will have a friend for a neighbor will be just perfect."

Allen just smiled. We all said goodbye, he went inside, and we continued our day.

All day long, I had to hear from Mum how she was glad I would have someone to look out for me and from Dad how there were many pretty girls here, and he would not be surprised if I didn't have a girlfriend by the time I came home for Christmas. I was so embarrassed from the interaction with Allen and now my parents' comments that I just wanted to hide under a rock and never come out again.

The rest of the trip was uneventful. There were no more run-ins with Allen and nothing my parents could embarrass me about. I met with an advisor and set my schedule for the fall before we left, and I received the information on how to order my books and collect them once I returned from Scotland for the semester. Then we headed home to get me packed and be back in the fall; it was such an exciting time. I know Mum and Dad had a blast, and I had meeting up and playing soccer with Allen to look forward to once I returned.

Chapter 5
MOVE-IN DAY

The rest of summer had flown by, and now it was move-in week. Mum had packed all of my bags, and Dad rented a van so we could take them all to the airport. I'd said my goodbyes to Grandad and Grandma. Plus, Samantha had stopped by to see me off before her parents drove her to her university for the semester. With all our goodbyes said and lugged packed, I loaded into the van, and off we went.

The drive to the airport could not have been more uneventful. Mum and Dad did not say much, and looking out the window to the fields as we drove by, I couldn't help but think to myself, *I will miss the beauty of this place, but I am glad to be heading to the start of my life.* We arrived at the terminal. Dad set off to get my luggage checked in while Mum and I got in line for check-in; the lines were long today, making me wonder how many other families were sending their children off to a university far from home. Would any of them be starting a new life like me, or would most of them be returning to their villages and living a simple life? This I knew I never wanted.

After we made it through the security line and were on our way to the gate, Dad said, "Our flight is not for some time. Would you like to get lunch with your mum and me?" I smiled, knowing he wanted to spend as much time with us as a family as possible because I wouldn't be home for such a long time. Plus, I was starving, so this worked out perfectly. We found a lovely little cafe in the terminal, had a light lunch, and talked and laughed about old memories from my childhood. It hurt me inside to know that I was leaving for reasons my parents did not know and that I was too afraid to tell them before I went, and even now, while everything was so perfect, I still couldn't do it.

The time had come to board our flight to Michigan, and we all showed excitement as we queued. Once on the plane and settled, Dad started talking to the man across the aisle, asking them their reasons for traveling to the States. They were going on holiday to see some family, and my father took it upon himself to let them and everyone know that he was traveling to send his son to one of the best universities in the country. This annoyed me, as I did not like the attention, and Dad was drawing so much to himself.

For most of the flight, I read a book on American history that I needed for one of my classes while Mum and Dad chatted with one another or slept. It was not a short flight, but I did not sleep much as I kept thinking about classes, seeing Allen again, making new friends, and finally figuring out who David Ricci was. As we started our descent, Mum and Dad, being the energetic people they are, started cleaning up the row we were in and making sure the new friends they had made were all taken care of, just being very much themselves. I put my books away and just sat there looking out the window, watching as we passed the clouds. The plane got closer to the ground, followed by the screeching of the tires as we touched down and the aircraft came to an unavoidable fast deceleration halt. Thankfully, my parents, as free and open as they are, were not those who clapped when a plane landed; I still to this day wonder why people clap. It's the pilot's job to land the plane.

The terminal was more of a zoo than back home, with people everywhere coming and going in all directions, trying to find gates for connecting flights or trying to find their way to the luggage claim. I have to say the airport here is a maze and one can easily get turned around. We made it down to the luggage claim area, and there was a massive crowd of people all waiting around the belts to collect their luggage. Dad and Mum took a spot, and Dad had me go down a little farther in case they missed one of my bags. I was standing there waiting for what felt like an eternity when a loud buzzing alarm sounded, and the belt started to move. One by one, bags began coming down the belt. Dad and Mum grabbed a few, but the mad rush of people behind us dashed for the belt, and it became a free-for-all to collect their luggage. I laughed to myself. *How barbaric*, I thought. We would all get our luggage much faster if we waited our turn. I grabbed the few bags my parents missed and headed for the doors to meet them by the car Dad had rented to drive us to my apartment.

When we arrived at the apartment, Dad did his best to find a place to park; I had never seen so many people trying to do the same thing at the same time. Once parked, we started to unload the bags and move them into my new place. Mum began to unpack, and I returned to get more luggage. Dad was talking to another parent when I arrived. "Oh, David!" He smiled. "Come here and meet Mr. and Mrs. Lombardi. They're from the same village as me, and their daughter, Alessia, is starting school here too and staying in the flat next to yours."

I smiled, walked over, and said hello. We chatted for a bit, and Alessia and I hit it off so well that we exchanged numbers in case we needed anything, being so far from home.

I turned to Dad and said, "Mum must be getting worried. I'm sure she's wondering where we are." Dad nodded and agreed. We said our goodbyes to the Lombardis and headed to the apartment to finish helping Mum unpack.

After we unpacked, Mum still felt the apartment needed homey touches. She asked Dad to take her to some shops, and I decided to stay behind and get things moved around to my liking. Now that I was alone, I texted Allen that I was back in the States and just getting moved in and settled into my new place. He responded that this was excellent news and we would have to go out to celebrate this weekend. I smiled, threw my phone down on the bed, and continued working on getting things in place. It was starting to get late, and Mum and Dad had still not returned, so I went to the apartment next door to check on Alessia and her parents. I knocked on the door and waited for an answer.

Alessia answered. "Oh David, how are you? Please come in. Mum and I are about to make something to eat. Dad went out to get some things."

I smiled and entered. Her flat was no different from mine in size and style, but hers seemed more cozy and comforting. Her mum was in the kitchen making something that smelled fantastic; Mum had tried cooking Italian food for Dad but never seemed to get it just right. Dad always appreciated Mum trying but said it would never be like home.

Alessia and I sat in the living area chatting when her mother called out, "Alessia, the supper is done. Would your friend like to stay?"

I smiled at her and said, "Thank you, Mrs. Lombardi, but Mum and Dad should be back soon, and I don't want to intrude on your family time." I stood up, thanked them for allowing me to spend time there, and headed for the door. Alessia walked with me back to my apartment and thanked me for spending time with her. She said she felt much more comfortable knowing she had someone to talk to. We said our goodbyes, and she walked back to her apartment down the hall. After she had entered her door I turned to go back into mine.

I entered the flat to find Mum and Dad had added lamps and rugs to the space and were hanging paintings on the walls of landscapes and other reminders of home; now it was starting to feel cozier like Alessia's place did. Mum looked up. "Oh, David, there you are. Dad and I were thinking we should go out to dinner tonight. I've always wanted to try sushi, and there's a place around the corner we saw while looking for shops."

I smiled. "Sure, Mum, we can do whatever you and Dad would like."

Mum smiled and expressed pure joy and happiness to try something new and spend more time with me before they headed back to Scotland.

Dinner was fun. Mum ordered about one of everything, and watching her face as she tried each dish was a good laugh. Dad was not daring enough to try any of it, but I liked it. Everything was perfect, and it was an excellent way to end our long move-in day and our last night as a family before they headed back to Scotland in the morning.

The following day, we were up early. Mum cooked a big breakfast for the three of us, and we didn't talk much as I think Mum didn't want to start crying from knowing we wouldn't see one another for a few months. I promised her I would phone often and come home for the Christmas holiday, but I know this was not easy for her. It was still lovely to sit there and be together.

After we finished breakfast and everything was cleaned up, Dad asked me to walk with him. We walked to a nearby park and found a nice bench. He took a small box out of his pocket, handed it to me, and then said, "This was my father's; it's the only thing I have of him. He gave it to me on my first day of university and told me it was special and only to be used for important events."

I opened the box to find an excellent and elegant watch. I studied it for a moment. Dad never spoke of his father; he didn't even like him, and now he was giving me the only thing he had of his, and it was important. I looked at my dad, who was waiting for my response. "It's wonderful, Dad; I will take care of it, but what makes it so important that I can only wear it for important events?"

He looked at me and smiled. "Well, you see, son, I have only worn it a handful of times. I wore it the day I met your mother, and I wore it the day we were married and the day you were born. My father told me when he gave it to me that it brings good luck, and every time I wore it, it was the luckiest day of my life." I could tell that this watch was invaluable to my father, and now he was trusting me with one of his most prized possessions. I thanked him for the gift, hugged him, and promised to protect it and only wear it when I needed luck and on special occasions. He smiled, and we walked back to my apartment.

Once back at the apartment, Mum and Dad packed their bags, and Dad took them down to the car while Mum and I said our goodbyes. I walked her to the car, hugged and kissed them both, and then watched them drive off. That was it; move-in was over, and Mum and Dad were gone. I was left alone for the first time. I felt sad to watch the car get smaller in the distance but also excited about what adventures awaited me in the coming weeks and months.

I headed back inside and ran into Alessia and her parents saying their goodbyes. I wished them safe travels back home as I passed them in the hall to my place and invited Alessia over for a chat and movie later, as I knew we both were going to be having our first night alone and figured she could use the company. I went inside so they could be alone, sat on the couch, and smiled.

I had done it; I could now be the honest David.

Chapter 6
PARTY

Later in the day, while I was sitting in the apartment still getting things put into place, I received a text from Allen. I opened it to read, *Party tomorrow, my home, Apt 5B @ 7. Bring whoever you like. See you then, Allen.* I texted Alessia and asked if she wanted to go with me, and she said yes.

The next night, around six, Alessia came to my place so we could get ready to go. She wore a bright-colored dress with flowers and some heels. I thought it odd one would get so dressed up for a party in someone's college apartment, but it's a thing people do, so I smiled and told her she looked charming. I wore dark blue jeans and a nice polo that Mum had bought me for class. We chatted briefly about the upcoming term and what lessons we would be taking. Alessia was ready to dive into her principal and the world of art; I was more practical and had stuck with core coursework for this semester such as maths and English.

The time was now seven. We didn't want to be the first ones there but also didn't want to be the last. We agreed to leave my apartment at 7:10. This way, we would still be pretty early but not right on time, and since we only had to go up one floor, it wasn't like we had a fair way to go.

When Alessia and I arrived at Allen's door, we could hear light music and chatter. I knocked, and a few moments later, Allen answered. "David, it's so good to see you. How are you settling in? And who is this lovely lady you brought with you?"

I smiled, one of those *I'm glad to see you too but in a much different way* smiles that you give to someone you have a crush on but are afraid to tell them. I said, "Yeah, settling in well, still trying to get things into place. This is Alessia. She lives next door to me, and we've hit it off."

Alessia smiled at Allen and gave him a playful "Hello." With that, Allen invited us in.

The inside of the apartment was full of people, much more than I expected so early in the evening. Alessia saw someone whom she'd met earlier in the week who was in the same program as her and went off to say hi and chat for a bit. I found a corner to stand in where I could observe what was going on but not make it too obvious that I was way out of my comfort zone.

Allen came over. He had a drink for me, and two other guys followed behind him. "David, this is Mark and Anthony; both of them are on my soccer team. I told them how we met and that you might be interested in joining us." I greeted both of them, and Allen took off to answer the door while Mark, Anthony, and I talked with one another about soccer and the upcoming term.

Mark was your typical jock type. He seemed to have played almost every sport he possibly could, was very muscular, and was even majoring in something sports-related, none of which I cared for, but he was still someone easy to chat with. Anthony was more intriguing to me. He was tall yet slender in build, had long dark brown hair, and was majoring in computer science, so how he came into sports was a mystery, nevertheless, his wit was charming and I could have spent the rest of the night talking to him, and I did.

Around elevenish, Alessia came up to me and said she'd had enough. I agreed that I was getting tired of being social as well, and we found Allen, thanked him for the invite, and started to head out. As we were leaving, Anthony walked up to us and asked, "Leaving already?"

I looked at him. "Yes, Alessia would like to go. We came together, and I was also getting tired, so we're bowing out."

He just looked at me; I wasn't sure if it was my accent or if he was thinking, wow, was a lame ass this guy is. He said, "Well, I was thinking of leaving too. I'll walk with you two." We both told him that wouldn't be necessary as we live one floor down, but he insisted, so we collected our things and headed out.

We dropped off Alessia at her apartment. I told her I would come over tomorrow, and we could chat about how the night went. She smiled and headed on into her place. Anthony and I walked on down to my apartment, and once there, I thanked him for chatting with me tonight and walking with us home.

He smiled and said, "It was nothing. I only went to the party to be near Mark, but he doesn't seem to notice me how I want him to."

I looked at him, puzzled. Then I said, "Not to pry, but you make it sound like you fancy Mark."

He smiled as he looked down to the ground. "Well, I do, but I know he's straight. The guys on the team know I'm gay, and they don't care at all, but I'm afraid of what they would think if they knew I liked Mark as more than a friend and teammate."

I frowned as this was just like me wanting to be on the team to be near Allen.

We stood silently for a minute before he said, "I shouldn't have said that; please don't tell anyone."

I smiled and said, "I promise not to tell anyone, and to be honest with you, the only reason I want to join the team is because I fancy Allen."

This shocked Anthony. "Allen," he said. "How could anyone like Allen?"

I was confused. Allen to me had a nice demeanor, and I didn't see why anyone wouldn't like him. I asked, "What's wrong with Allen?"

Anthony looked at me and frowned. "It's not my place to say or spread rumors, but I would be careful around him. He's a nice guy but has a past that some find less than desirable."

I just gave him a half smile as I wasn't sure if he was telling the truth or if he fancied him as well as Mark and was trying to get me uninterested so he could have him all to himself.

Quickly, I changed the subject to computer science, as I was becoming very uncomfortable and didn't want to hear any more about Allen being a bad guy. Hearing I was interested in computer science made Anthony cheer up. I invited him in, and we talked until well past two about school, life, and our feelings about liking men and how we'd managed them up to this point. It was nice having someone I could talk to about this. The only other person who knew was Samantha, and we hadn't spoken about it since I told her I was interested in men.

Finally, around three, we both agreed it was time to call it a night. I asked him, "Do you have a long way to get home?"

Anthony responded, "Just the other side of campus, about a three-mile walk."

I knew a walk like that was not very far, but it was three in the morning, and I felt terrible that I had kept him all this time, so I offered, "Well, you can sleep on the couch if you want. I mean it's late, and I would feel bad if something happened."

Anthony smiled. "Oh, it's not a problem at all; I've done it before. Besides, since we just met, I don't want to intrude on you." He collected his things, and I walked him to the door. At the door, we hugged and thanked each other for the chat and for being able to vent. As he prepared to turn and leave, Anthony gave me a sidelong devilish smile and said, "Next time, if you want me to stay, instead of offering the couch, offer a side of the bed."

I just stared, unsure of what to say. He laughed to make sure I knew it was a joke, then walked down the hall towards the exit.

Once the door was shut and locked, I went to my room, changed out of the jeans and polo, and got into my pajamas. Sitting in bed, I could not get his comment out of my head. Was he joking or being serious? Could someone be that blunt with what they wanted? My mind buzzed about this, and then I started to think about his comment earlier in the night about Allen. What was it about him that Anthony knew that I didn't, and should I be worried? All I knew was I had a lot to discuss with Alessia tomorrow, and maybe I should give Samantha a ring to see how she was doing at her school and what she thought. I drifted off to sleep.

The next morning, I woke to a text from Alessia saying she had something to tell me. I got ready and headed over to her apartment. I knocked and could hear her running for the door. "David, thank goodness you're here. Please come in. I have an amazing story from last night I wanna share with you." I entered, and she led me over to the couch, and we sat down, looking at each other. She went on, "So last night at the party, when I was talking to my friend, that guy Mark you were talking to approached me and gave me his number and said to text him sometime." I looked at her, waiting to see where this was going. She continued, "So anyway, I couldn't sleep last night once I got back home, so I texted him, and we talked most of the night, and he asked me to go on a date with him today for lunch."

I smiled and said, "Alessia, that's fantastic. I'm so happy for you." I felt happiness for my friend, but in the back of my head, I was sad for Anthony as I knew he liked Mark, and now here I was, telling my other friend how excited I was for her.

We talked about what she was planning on wearing, and after helping her pick out an outfit that she thought would be appropriate but also a little flirty, we walked down to the entrance of our building, where Mark was waiting for her. "Oh David, hi, I didn't know you knew Alessia."

"Yeah, we live next to each other. Nice to see you again; I hope you have a good time." Alessia hugged me goodbye, and they headed out for their date. I went inside as I was still tired, lay down in bed, and tried my hardest to go back to sleep.

Later in the day, I heard a knock on my door. It was Alessia. She gave me and hug and had a big smile on her face, I knew from this that the date must have gone well. "Can I come in?" she asked.

"Oh, of course, please come in," I said as I let her in the door. "So...how was your date?" I asked, trying to seem interested but still torn between Alessia and Anthony.

She sat on the couch and said, "Everything was wonderful. Mark is such a nice guy. I think I like him, and I think he likes me as well."

I just sat there looking without saying anything and waited for her to continue.

"We went to a small coffee shop on campus and just had the most pleasant conversation about life and our plans for the future. And I know this sounds crazy, but I want him in my future if possible."

I looked at her with an incredulous stare. Alessia picked up on my doubts. "I know you think I'm crazy for saying so, but I've never met someone as passionate as him, and I'm from Italy," she said playfully.

I smiled and said, "I'm happy you had such a good time, and I hope things work out for you. Just be careful, okay?"

Alessia smiled, stood up, gave me a hug for understanding, and said she needed to go home and get ready for classes tomorrow. I walked out into the hall with her and watched as she made her way down the hall to her apartment, and then I went back inside to get my things ready for the following day.

Chapter 7
FIRST DAY OF CLASSES

The first day of classes had arrived, and I was up early, excited about my courses this semester—so early that I was up at 6:00 a.m. My first class was at 9:30, but I wanted to ensure I had time to get ready and find my way to the building and classroom with time to spare. I picked out one of the shirts Mum had bought me for classes and a pair of jeans, put on my runners, grabbed my backpack, and headed out the door around 8:00.

The campus was alive and busy, with many people going in all directions to find where their classes were. I knew how to get to the building of my first class, but finding the room itself once inside was going to be a challenge. Once inside, I looked at the paper I had with my classes written down and the room numbers, then looked for an information board to try and find my way. While looking at the board, I heard a voice behind me. "David, hi."

I turned around to see Mark standing there. "Oh, hello, Mark, how are you?" I asked to be polite.

"I'm well, just heading to class. What are you looking for?" he asked with a tone that seemed like he wanted to help, but there was also maybe some other motive.

"I'm looking for room 303; I have maths this morning."

Mark looked at me for a second before he said, "Well, what luck, I'm heading there too. It looks like we have class together, but I've never heard anyone call it maths."

I smiled, but deep down, I felt embarrassed that he'd called me out for how I said it. "Well, in the UK we call it maths, and I'm just so used to it that I forget there's no S here."

Mark could tell I was embarrassed and apologized, saying he didn't mean to offend. I told him it was okay, and we headed up the stairs to the third floor to find room 303 for our first class.

The classroom was different from what I was expecting; this was a massive room with 100 seats. I didn't think maths would be held in such a large lecture hall, but I was okay with this as it meant I could blend into the crowd and not have to worry about being called on by the professor. Mark and I sat in the middle of the back row so that we would be able to see the lecture screen. About fifteen minutes later, the room started to fill up with the others in the class and was almost full in no time. I could hear everyone digging in their bags to get out laptops, textbooks, and notebooks, with some quiet chatter between people taking this class with friends. I leaned over to Mark. "Are all classes like this?" I asked.

He just chuckled. "Well, some classes are about this size, some are much smaller, and some can be much bigger; it just depends. You'll get used to it."

A few moments later, an older gentleman walked into the room and headed for the lecture podium. He was a short man, probably only about five feet in height, but as soon as he walked in, almost everyone stopped talking and watched him as he got set up. "Good morning," he said softly in a monotone voice, one of those voices that you just knew would be tedious to listen to this early in the morning. Most of the class said good morning back, and he went into the lecture without skipping a beat.

After about fifteen minutes, Mark leaned over to me and said, "My god, if he were any more dull, you would think the book itself was teaching us."

I smiled and tried not to laugh at his comment but fully agreed. I leaned over and said, "I've seen more excitement from a sheep on the farm than this guy is giving us."

Mark must have pictured me back on the farm in Scotland as he busted out laughing. It was so loud the whole room was now looking up at us, even the professor. Mark did not seem to care; he just said, "Sorry, please continue."

On the other hand, I was mortified, but the small professor seemed to be used to things like this. He commented: "Some of us find great humor in math, as we just saw, but others find it dull and boring. Anyway, let's get back to it." He returned to his lecture like nothing had caused a significant disturbance. The rest of the class was uneventful; Mark and I did not dare to make any more comments to each other for fear of causing another outburst of laughter.

Once class was over and we were heading out of the hall, I did not know what came over me, but I blurted out, "So, how was the date with Alessia?"

Mark looked at me with a face of surprise that I had asked. It took me less than a second to realize I might have said something I shouldn't have. I thought, *Oh shit, I just shouldn't have said that; we don't know one another that well, and he knows Alessia and I are friends.* Now I was panicking as Mark was staring.

I felt like I should say something, and just as I was about to open my mouth, Mark spoke. "Everything was very nice. She and I had a really good time together. I'm going to ask her out again. Do you think she would say yes?"

I smiled and nodded in approval. Mark took that as a yes, and we continued to walk down the hall talking. Mark then mentioned Anthony and how he'd been acting weird towards him lately and asked if he had mentioned anything to me. I didn't know if I should say anything about what Anthony and I had talked about a few nights ago. Mark stated, "I know he has feelings for me, and I have told him many times that I'm not into guys, but he will not give it up."

I looked at him. "Why is that?" I asked, curious to know more about Anthony and why he had made it so clear to be careful around Allen.

"Well, that's kind of a touchy subject. He, Allen, and I all went out after soccer one-night last year, and we got a little too deep in our drinks if you know what I mean. Anthony decided to try his luck and kissed me, and I didn't stop him. Then he tried Allen, who didn't take it as well and punched him in the jaw." He paused. "Ever since then, our friendship has been strained. He's hung up on me for not stopping him, and his and Allen's relationship has suffered too."

I looked at him in disbelief that Allen would have hit Anthony over a kiss. I think Mark noticed this as he said, "Allen is not homophobic or anything. I believe the amount of alcohol and being caught off guard caused him to do it. He's tried to let Anthony know he's sorry, but he won't hear it and makes it a point to tell everyone about it."

I just smiled sympathetically. From there, we parted ways as our next class was in opposite directions. Walking down the hall, I ran into Allen, almost knocking him over. "Oh my god, Allen, I'm so sorry. Are you okay?"

He turned around with a thunderous look on his face, but when he saw it was me, his expression changed. "Oh, David, I'm all right. You might want to be more careful; I was about to turn around and have a fight with whoever was being so rude, so good thing I saw it was you before I did." He laughed, trying to make light of the situation.

I, on the other hand, was shitting myself from my conversation with Mark. "Yeah, I should be looking up when walking down the halls, huh?" I said to get this interaction over. We laughed it off, and I continued down the hall to my next class.

The rest of my day was uneventful; my other professors were much more lively than the one in my maths class and made for an enjoyable day. I met some incredible people in my classes and was starting to feel less self-conscious about my accent. Everyone was much more accepting and open-minded than I initially thought. I had heard from others about how all Americans are rude and don't take kindly to people, not from here, but I didn't experience any of this aside from some people asking what a specific word meant, and I was okay with that.

On my way back to my apartment building, I saw Alessia was waiting for me outside. "David, hi. How was your day?"

I smiled. "Today was eventful. How was yours?"

Alessia stared at me with the most enthusiastic grin I had ever seen. "Oh my god, David, it was amazing. First, I love all of my courses, and second, Mark texted me and asked me out again. Today was perfect."

I grinned, knowing well that Mark was going to ask her out again. Before I could respond, Alessia said, "Oh, Mark also told me you two have math together and that you made him laugh so hard that you guys made the whole lecture stop. Good for you, glad to hear you're making friends and having fun."

I laughed. "Yeah, he and I made a name for ourselves in class today, and yeah, it's nice to be making friends." We walked to our hall together, said our goodbyes, and entered our apartments.

Once inside, I could not stop thinking about Allen hitting Anthony and how I ran straight into him. I felt like an idiot. How could I be attracted to such a mean-spirited person? I tried to clear it from my mind. I cooked myself something to eat, then sat on the couch and started working on my homework for the evening while eating my supper. No matter what happened between Anthony and Allen, the fact that he did not turn around and start swinging at me in the hall today made me think that he was not as bad as they were making him seem. *Is there something I'm missing?* I wondered as I read my history book on the 1500s.

Once done with my classwork, I stuffed everything back into my bookbag before I went into the bedroom, got my things for a shower, headed into the bathroom, took my shower, brushed my teeth, and went right to bed, as today had taken a lot out of me. I wanted to sleep for the next day, and since I only had classes in the afternoon, I did not need to rush. I just lay in bed, thinking about Anthony and wondering why I managed to run into everyone else today but him and why he and Mark were so set on making sure people watched out around Allen. I'd seen his temper for myself. Still, I also noticed that he had some self-control as he didn't beat me into the ground once he saw it was me and not some random person. At the same time, it would not have been good for him to do that to someone unexpected, but he did control himself. All of this kept me up for a while before I was able to fall asleep.

Chapter 8
DATE

The next day, I woke to my phone ringing. I looked at it to see Anthony's name. "Hello," I answered in a not-fully-awake voice.

"David, hi. Did I wake you?"

I just rolled my eyes, knowing that he couldn't see. "No, I needed to get up anyway. What's up?"

I could hear him breathing on the phone, but he wasn't saying anything.

"Anthony, are you there?" I asked.

"Yeah, I'm here. Hey, listen... Would you like to go on a date with me?" he asked in a shy voice.

This took me aback. I remembered the first night we met, how good of a talk we had, and his comment that if I wanted him to stay to offer a side of my bed, but I didn't think he had any interest in me. "Umm, yeah, that would be fun," I said, trying not to make it clear I was uncertain.

"Oh great, I'll come by your place today after classes, and we can go out to this restaurant by your place that I like."

I smiled. "Sounds good, Anthony. I'll see you tonight." I hung up the phone, rolled onto my back, put my hands onto my face, and groaned loudly, thinking, *Why did I say yes?*

I jumped out of bed and called Samantha.

"Hello?"

Hearing Sam's voice put a smile on my face. "Sam, hi, are you free to talk?" I asked.

"Oh my god, David, I have time. How is America? Are you making friends? What about school? Tell me everything."

The enthusiasm in her voice made me smile; how I missed our daily walk and talks around the village. "Everything is fantastic here," I said. "We can discuss that soon, but I need your advice. I'm desperate and need to talk to someone."

"Let's hear it. I'll always give you my opinion, just like you always will for me."

I smiled as I knew this was true, which was one reason we were such good friends. "Well...I was just asked out by a guy here, and I said yes, but I think it might have been a mistake."

There was a pause. Did she not know what to say? Or had I blown her mind? She had only known I was into guys for a few months, and I still wasn't sure how she felt about it.

"David, that's fantastic. Why do you think it was a mistake?"

I thought momentarily. "Well, I don't like him back. I'm crushing on this other guy, but two people have told me now that I need to be careful around him, so I don't know." I could not see her face, but I knew she was rolling her eyes at the thought of me going after a guy I had no clue liked me back and that others were warning me about.

"Well, the way I see it, David, here is a guy who wants to get to know you better, and you never know, you might find that you like him back. There's no way to know unless you give it a chance. As for the other guy, you need to let go of it, love; if he's shown no interest and others are warning you about him, I think you shouldn't go down that path."

I hated that she was right, but I didn't want to admit it.

"Anyway, love, I have class, but call me back later today. I want to hear about your adventure in America."

I smiled, we said our goodbyes and hung up.

After talking with Sam, I thought, well, maybe she was right. I might enjoy myself. At least with Anthony, I knew he was gay. He wouldn't try to hit me for it like Allen did Anthony when he wanted to kiss him, and it was true Allen had shown no interest in guys, so maybe I should stop crushing over him and try to find someone else. I agreed that this would be good, got out of bed, and started getting ready for my classes.

Classes were uneventful, and only a little went on. I couldn't stop thinking about my date tonight with Anthony; I didn't hear anything my professors were lecturing about, and frankly, I didn't care. It's not like I was missing much; most were discussing the schedule and syllabus anyway. Once classes were over, I headed straight home to shower and get ready for my date with Anthony.

The time was now 5:00 p.m., and I was starting to wonder if Anthony was even coming or if this was some sick joke he was playing on me. Just then, my phone rang. I looked at it to see Alessia's name and answered, "Alessia, hello, how are you?"

She sounded excited to hear from me, saying, "Oh, David, I just wanted to call to ask where do you think I should go with Mark on our second date? Since we already had coffee, maybe we could try a restaurant next. What do you think?"

I smiled. Here was Alessia having the time of her life and being all excited about her date with Mark, while I was sitting here, nervous about my date that might or might not be happening. "Well, there are some great restaurants around the corner from here. Mum, Dad, and I had a great time at the sushi restaurant during move-in; you might like that. I'm going to a new place tonight with someone and can let you know what I think of it. They should be here any minute."

I could hear Alessia holding in her excitement. "David, you have a date? That's wonderful; I cannot wait to hear all about it. I'll let you go so you can get ready, and yeah, maybe one of the restaurants around the corner will be a great idea."

We said our goodbyes and hung up.

Fifteen minutes later, there was a knock on the door, and my heart started to race. I had never really made a big deal about my anxiety, but now I was having a full-on panic attack about who was waiting on the other side. I walked over, trying to calm myself before I got there. I sucked it up and pulled the door wide open. To my surprise, Allen was standing there.

"Oh Allen, hey, what's up?"

He looked just as surprised as I did. "Oh, hey, David. Sorry to stop by unannounced; I wanted to see if you wanted to hang out tonight."

Inside, I was screaming yes. Here was the guy I fancied the most, and now he was asking to hang out. *Why does the universe hate me so much right now?* I smiled, but inside I was mad that I knew I couldn't say yes with Anthony maybe on his way.

I looked at him and frowned. "I would, but unfortunately I already have plans for tonight."

He looked at me for a moment without saying anything.

"I'm free the rest of this week; we can try to hang out sometime then," I added.

He smiled at this and said, "Oh no, it's cool; let's try for later this week. Have fun tonight. Mark is with Alessia, and Anthony is not answering my texts, so I guess it's just me and my cat kind of night."

I smiled and agreed, and with that, he turned and headed down the hall to the stairs to head up to his unit.

I couldn't get the comment that Anthony was not responding out of my head; from what I knew about him, this was not typical and made me worry that he was hurt. I decided to text him and make sure he was all right.

Hey Anthony, I'm excited for tonight. Allen just stopped by and mentioned you had not answered his texts. Are you okay?

I sat there with my phone in my hand, waiting for the text notification to go off. There was a silence that felt like it was going on forever, but in reality, it was only about five minutes before my phone buzzed.

Hey David, I'm also excited about tonight. I'm almost there. Yeah, I've been ignoring him as I didn't want him to know you and I are going out tonight. I was afraid he would want to tag along, and then we couldn't have a real date.

I smiled; this was going to happen. I was going on a date, and while he was not my ideal guy, Anthony seemed decent enough, and I was starting to get over my anxiety. He must have been outside the building when he sent that message, as not even a moment later, he was knocking at my door. I quickly opened the door and invited him in. We chatted for a bit and discussed what kind of food we were in the mood for, the two of us came to an agreement to go to a small Mexican place on the other side of town so that there was a smaller chance of running into Allen, Mark, or Alessia.

The dinner was perfect, and the conversation was pleasant; while Anthony could hold a conversation, he spent much time talking about his degree and computers and how IT was an integral part of life. I hoped to hear more about him and his background, but otherwise, the date was going well.

Halfway through dinner, a young woman came into the restaurant, she noticed Anthony and headed over to our table. "Oh Anthony, hi, what are you doing here?" She did not even look at me and see we were in the middle of our dinner.

Anthony looked annoyed. "I'm here with my friend David. We're just having dinner and chatting about life."

I was shocked that he had just lied about this being a date. I knew he was out to people, but why was this woman different? I started to feel sick, and while I was not out, I couldn't help but feel bad that he lied about why we were together. She looked over and glared at me. She didn't introduce herself or ask my name. Then she looked at Anthony and said, "Oh, well, excuse me for interrupting." She walked off to the counter, collected her order, and walked out.

The rest of dinner was awkward. I tried to ask about her, but Anthony kept changing the subject. All of this made me feel bad about myself more and more, and I started to go into the dark place in my mind that I would get into when I allowed my low self-esteem and anxiety to get the best of me. I hadn't felt this lousy since graduation when I had to give the speech.

When we were done, and the waiter came with the check, I went for it, but Anthony said he would cover dinner to make up for the unpleasantness that happened in the second half. I tried to convince him to split it, but he would not allow it, so I offered to stop somewhere for dessert afterward; he agreed and paid the bill.

After walking around town and passing an ice cream parlor, I suggested we go in for our dessert. Anthony laughed, and we went in. The parlor was charming and designed to look like an old-fashioned soda shop, and the counter had all the tubs to pick from. We ordered and sat down. By this point, I was so in my thoughts I just blurted out, "We have to talk about dinner. I'm uncomfortable and think we need to address what happened."

Anthony looked at me and sighed. "Fine, you're right; I'm sorry. She's my ex, and we didn't have a great breakup."

I looked at him, confused. "Your ex? I thought you were gay?"

He looked at me. "Oh, I am...but I struggled with it for a few years and tried to date women. It was a disaster."

I sat there and smiled, as I knew what it was like to feel like that, wanting to be your true self but not knowing how to manage it and keep the peace. "Well, why did you lie and not tell her we were on a date? Do you not like me that way or are you embarrassed by being out with the foreign student with the accent?"

Anthony frowned. "I'm sorry I didn't tell her we were on a date. I feared it would get back to Mark and Allen, and I didn't want to put you through that."

I was upset with myself that I accused him of being embarrassed by me, but it was sweet that he was trying to protect me from Mark and Allen; whatever he meant about that. I was still unsure what this issue was with Allen. I smiled. "Well, I'm having a great time even with the unpleasantness from dinner, and I find it sweet you're looking out for me."

We finished our ice cream and started to walk back to my place.

During our walk back, Anthony was more interesting than at dinner. He told me about his religious parents, and how when he came out, it was this big ordeal that changed things for a few years but that everything was good now, and if we continued to go out and like one another he hoped to introduce me to them one day. I cringed at this idea in my mind. I was not mentally prepared to tell my parents, let alone meet the parents of someone I wasn't even in a serious relationship with, but I kept that to myself and just agreed so as not to make things even more awkward after dinner had been. When we arrived back at my place, I invited Anthony up, and we sat in the living room and chatted for a while before Anthony's phone started to ring, and he took a call. I tried not to listen but couldn't help it.

"Hey. Sorry, I've been busy today." There was a long pause as the person on the other side talked. "Oh, I'm just hanging out with a friend." *There he goes again. Wasn't this a date? Does everyone in the States not tell anyone they're on dates here?* I sat there getting more down as this was the second time tonight that he hadn't wanted to tell someone we were on a date.

Once he was off the phone, I was upset and wanted the night to end, so I said, "I need to get some sleep. I have class in the morning but I had a great time."

Anthony looked at his watch. "Oh yeah, it is getting late; I should get going anyway." He got his coat and headed for the door, then said, "I had a good time tonight, and I wouldn't mind doing this again sometime."

I just smiled and said, "Yeah." I closed the door and put my head against the wall. That was not the first date I was hoping for.

I showered and changed into my pajamas but was not tired. I could not stop thinking about how horribly wrong things had gone tonight. In the beginning, I had started to think I might like Anthony, but his not wanting anyone to know we were on a date or even that we had gone on one made me feel bad about myself and depressed, like maybe I was not able to be liked or loved by anyone. Perhaps it would be better if I just kept to myself here, just like I did back home. I just lay there thinking about how it made me feel when I rolled over and looked at the clock. It was only 10:30, which wasn't late at all, but my excuse that it was late had worked, and Anthony didn't protest at all. Why was he so determined to leave when the last time we spoke, he stuck around for hours, and we lost track of time. Why was today different?

After some time, I let my mind get the better of me and thought I had to have done something wrong. I wanted to call Sam, but it was now 3:30 a.m., and I didn't want to wake her. But I needed to talk to someone. I could text Allen and see if he wanted to come down. But no, I did not want to put him in between Anthony and me, plus I still liked him and did not want to make it awkward between us, so I texted Alessia.

The date started okay, then took a bizarre turn, all in my feelings about it...David.

Alessia must have been waiting for my text as she replied in an instant. *Be right over, bringing snacks.* A few moments later, there was knocking on the door. I opened it and let Alessia in. She smiled, walked over to the coffee table, and dumped all kinds of food onto it: chips, cookies, drinks, and other comfort foods that one would eat when one had a breakup or a bad day. We put on a romantic comedy and started to dig in.

Sitting there eating and watching the movie was helping me calm down, but then Alessia spoke. "So...are we going to talk about this disaster date or what?"

I started to panic again. I did not know how to tell her I went out with Anthony and that he treated me poorly, but I knew I had to say something. "I don't know...it was weird. We were sitting there having a good time when this girl came up out of nowhere and started being a complete weirdo to my date."

Alessia looked at me, waiting for more, I did not say anything else and was just staring back at her. "Hmmm...it sounds like you may be leaving some information out there, David."

I knew I had to tell her about how Anthony lied and said nothing about it being a date and that she was an ex, and I guessed starting by saying it was an ex would be safe. "Well, it turned out that this girl was my date's ex and she was mad about something, but I never did figure out what." I anxiously waited to see if Alessia would put together what I had just said. With each passing second, my heart raced.

"Oh, David, you should be careful dating bisexual women. They can be a handful. My best friend back home is bi, and she was always getting into trouble."

I smiled. "Well, the bigger issue is that my date also told this girl that we were just friends out to eat, and when I questioned why that was, I was not given a very good explanation, but I blew it off as I didn't think it was that big of a deal."

Alessia looked at me like I was a complete idiot. "David, honey." There was a long pause. "You shouldn't blow that off; what kind of person wants to take someone out then, when seen in public with them, act like they're not on a date? If I were you, I would call her up, demand an explanation, and tell her if you ever want to see each other again, it better be the truth." This preceded another long pause while she took a bite of cookie dough. "I mean, if Mark tried to pull something like that, I would make a big deal right in the middle of the restaurant before walking out on his ass, and you should do the same with her."

Everything she said made sense, but I didn't know how to do that with Anthony, as I knew soccer was starting soon, and I didn't want it to be more awkward than it already was. So I said, "You're right. I'll be sure to address it the next time we talk to each other."

Alessia smiled, and we continued to watch the movie before we eventually both passed out.

When I awoke the following day, Alessia was still sleeping on the other end of the couch. I got up and started to make breakfast. When she woke, I heard, "What time is it, and who is in my kitchen?"

I laughed. "Well, good morning. It's nine-thirty, and it's my kitchen; we passed out after binge-eating and watching romantic comedies."

Alessia shot up and looked around before realizing who was talking and that she was, in fact, not in her apartment. "Oh, thank god, David, I was about to have a heart attack wondering who this man was in my apartment and how he got in... So tell me, this date you had, what was her name? You never mentioned it last night."

I started to panic. "It's not important," I said.

Alessia would not accept that as an answer. "Oh NO," she said. "You're not getting off that easy."

I started feeling sick and anxious again, but she would not give up, and I figured I could trust her. I did need someone to talk to about these things, as it would not always be easy to talk to Sam about it. "Okay, fine, I'll tell you, but you have to promise not to tell anyone, not even Mark, understand?" I said in a firm voice, while on the inside, I was having a full-on panic attack.

"Oh my god, yes, I understand. She must be important to the guys if you don't want them to find out," she said, looking as if I was about to say I stole a girl from Mark, Allen, or Anthony.

"Well, first, my date was with a guy, not a girl," I said in a shaky voice, half expecting her to throw a fit.

Not fazed by this, Alessia asked, "Was it Allen?"

I looked at her and then said, "What would make you think I went on a date with Allen, and why are you not surprised?" I asked in a confused manner.

She laughed and said, "Oh, David, sweetie, I knew you were gay the day we met during move-in; that's why I brought all this food last night. I knew how this would go, and as for Allen, you clearly want that man. Mark and I always talk about it."

I felt sick. Mark thought I liked Allen, and they talked about it. Did Allen think so, too? I looked at Alessia and said, "Well, most are surprised; when I told friends back home, they were shocked, and no, my date was not Allen. I'm sure he's straight."

She laughed harder now. "Well, you might be right about Allen; I was taking a shot in the dark. As for people being shocked, oh honey, the world is much more open and accepting than your small village in Scotland; people can tell these things when not sheltered from life. Now, if it wasn't Allen and this date was horrible, and I can't tell Mark about it, who did you go on a date with?"

I was not feeling as confident that it was okay to be my authentic self as Alessia was suggesting and deep down I knew I would continue to hide who I was, but there was no getting out of telling her I went out with Anthony, so I said, "Well...my date was with...it was with..."

Alessia interrupted, "David, it's okay, you can tell me."

I smiled. "It was with Anthony," I blurted out.

She sat there, not saying anything, just staring. My heart was racing fast, like a horse running at full speed. Minutes passed before she spoke. "Oh David, Anthony, sweetie, I know you're new to all this, but honey, if he's gonna lie about being on a date with you and wants to hide it from the others, he's not the right one."

I knew she was right, but I didn't know how to be my authentic self. I agreed with her, we had breakfast, and she headed home to get ready for her day. Just then my phone buzzed; it was a text from Anthony.

Sorry about last night. I want to make it up to you xoxo.

I did not respond and instead finished getting ready to head out to my classes for the day.

Chapter 9
SOCCER PRACTICE

The rest of the week after that night was pretty relaxed; nothing exciting happened in my classes. Mark did not mention anything to me in maths the following day, so I assumed Alessia kept her promise not to tell him about Anthony and me. Soon the weekend was here, and practice was meant to start for soccer. I was still having trouble calling it that and would still say football and get confused looks from people when they figured out I was not talking about American football. That morning, I put my cleats in my bag with all my other gear and headed out the door to meet Allen at the front of the building. We agreed to walk to the field together to compensate for not hanging out the other night.

Once at the field, Allen had to set up. Anthony saw us walk in together and came running over with a look of panic. Once he'd made it over to me, he said, "You didn't tell him about us, did you?"

I stared at him disbelievingly before saying, "Of course not. Why would I?" My tone made it clear I was still upset with how things had gone the other night and that we hadn't talked since, and now he was again worried about people knowing.

"Oh, good, I just don't want to see you hurt," he said. All I could do was think he didn't care about that, only what they thought of him. We chatted for a bit more about soccer and how we hoped the season would go when Mark came walking over to us. He had a grin on his face, one that said *I know something*

I shouldn't, and it's killing me not to say. Once he made it over to us, he was pleasant and was asking about what positions we wanted to play, but he kept looking at me like he was about to explode; all I could think was Alessia had told him, and now I was panicking that something terrible was about to happen, and I started to feel dizzy. I quickly sat down.

Mark noticed and asked, "Are you all right, David?"

I smiled. "Yeah, I just figured I would sit till we start."

He and Anthony shrugged and walked off to finish setting up. I texted Alessia to ask if she told Mark, and she said no, so why was he acting so weird?

A few moments later, everything was set up, and we started to practice. The other guys on the team were a group looking to find something to do; no one else knew them, but everyone seemed to get along well. Everyone found a position they would be best at. I ended up in a defensive position, which I was okay with as this meant I could not be the start on the field, and I preferred that. Mark ended up as one of the goalies, which made sense as he was a tall, well-built guy who blocked most of the net; Anthony and Allen were both forwards. The practice was uneventful, and everything seemed to be okay; Anthony did not seem worried about our date, and I was starting to relax and let my guard down until, during a break, Allen and Mark suggested that after practice, the four of us should hang out. I was okay with this, but Anthony started acting weird about it and trying to make up a reason why that would not be smart. He was outvoted by Mark and Allen.

Anthony then pulled me over to a tall tree out of view and said, "Look, I'm sorry about the other night, and I want to make it up to you. I like you, I do, and I think you like me, but I don't want those two finding out, so can we give this a try but keep it secret from them?"

I stood there, stunned. Did he say he liked me and wanted to try and make us work? My mind was racing, and I knew I had to say something. I wished I could call Sam and get her opinion, but that was not an option. Anthony was staring at me, and he wanted an answer now. Finally, I said, "I would like that." I felt like an idiot, but Anthony smiled and leaned over and kissed me. That was more than I could handle; my anxiety was now at unsafe levels. I felt dizzy, like I was going to pass out. I put my hand on his shoulder to keep my balance, and we sat there for a minute before we heard someone coming. We soon gathered ourselves. Anthony headed off, and I stayed behind in a daze. My mind was racing. Did all of that happen? Why was I so worked up over this, and why did I start to have a panic attack? I knew I had to get back. We had our first game in a week, and this would be our only practice; while I thought this was a lousy idea, I knew I had no say. I gathered my thoughts and headed back to the field.

The rest of practice, I was lost in thought about what had happened with Anthony moments before, how it seemed we were on a path to being an actual legitimate couple, but also that I could not see why he was so against going out with Mark and Allen after practice. Then it hit me: Anthony tried to kiss them both one night after soccer; was he worried he would try it again? With all of this buzzing in my head, I was not paying attention, and I took a ball right to the side of my head. *Bam*, as it hit me, and I fell to the ground. For a moment, I just lay there before I realized what had happened. As I looked up to the group of guys standing around me to make sure I was all right, I knew I had to say something to not look like a complete idiot, so what did I do? I spoke with the thickest accent I had, the one I tried to hide as best I could but knew would make them laugh and let them know I was okay. "Blimey, who let the ram on the field? I thought I was back in Scotland for a second there." With those words, everyone burst into laughter. Allen helped me to my feet, and everyone agreed it was a good time to end the practice.

Once packed up, Mark and Allen tried to find a place for us to go while Anthony tried to protest the four of us hanging out. This annoyed me inside. I wanted to go out with the guys; I needed new mates, and I also wanted to spend more time with Anthony to see if this was going anywhere. I stayed quiet as even the thought of giving my two cents made me uneasy. Eventually, Anthony gave in, and we headed to what the guys called an "Irish pub." While I am not a snob in any manner, when someone says a pub, I think of the ones back home on the street corners with witty names where men sit down after a long day to have a pint or four with their mates before heading home to their family. This place had none of that; the name was a generic Irish last name, and the front looked like it was trying to resemble the streets of Ireland but was in the center of a busy street with restaurants and shops all around.

Once inside, we waited to be seated, and once we sat down, the guys started talking about the day and practice and how things went, including the ball I took to the face and called a ram. The time was pleasant; we ordered lots of food and talked, and they drank. I, not yet of age, couldn't drink and did not care either. I was old enough to drink back home, but in America, I was not. I found this silly as I could buy a gun here or smoke, but I couldn't drink; how backward I sometimes thought America was. I noticed that Anthony started to get more anxious during dinner when Mark and Allen got up to walk to the bar. I leaned over and asked, "Are you okay? You seem to be getting very uncomfortable."

He looked at me with a face of terror before saying, "I just really did not want to come out with the guys; aside from the first night we met in Allen's apartment, we haven't hung out since I got drunk and tried to kiss Allen, and he punched me for it."

This took me aback; they all seemed to be such good mates, and now I was being told they didn't even talk to one another, but then I remembered what Allen said to me the night of mine and Anthony's date, that he tried reaching out to him, and Anthony had not responded. And Anthony told me it was because of our time together, so was that just another one of his lies? How many more lies had he told me? I wanted to ask, but Mark and Allen were now back, and I didn't want to make it awkward.

The rest of the night went on with no more issues. Anthony was showing signs of relaxing, and I was starting to feel more comfortable until Mark said, "So, David, Alessia tells me you had a date, but she won't tell me anything about it. All she said was you didn't have a good time, and your date ended up being a tosser. Did I use that right? Tosser?"

I froze. How in the bloody hell was I to explain my date without giving up details on who I went with and that he was not sitting next to me at this very moment? And now Mark had just told him I hated our date and then called him a tosser. There was so much going on in my head; first, how dare he call me out like that, and second, don't use a word like tosser just because I'm from the UK. I glanced over to Anthony, who also had a look of panic on his face.

Thankfully Allen said, "Hey now, Mark, you know the rules; we don't talk about personal matters after soccer. We made that rule the night of the incident."

I looked over at them in confusion. "The incident?" I asked. With that, Anthony was up and dashed away from the table. I turned my attention to the other two, then asked, "Does this have to do with the time he got drunk and kissed you both, and you hit him, Allen?" I instantly regretted asking, but now it was out in the open, and I could tell everyone was uncomfortable. They looked at each other and nodded.

"Well," Mark said, "I guess if you're going to be in our friend group, it's time we came clean about the whole thing. Anthony doesn't talk to us outside of some parties and soccer. While we know about his sexuality, and have no issue with it, he gets into these moods where he feels everyone is out to get him or homophobic, Allen and myself included." There was a long pause. While sitting there, I tried to process this as fast as possible. Mark said, "When Anthony and I told you that you need to be careful around Allen, it wasn't because we think he's a bad guy, well, I don't, at least, but the night when Anthony kissed us both..."

Another long pause this time, and then Allen spoke. "Look, we know that you're not straight, and we don't care, and we can sense there's something between you and Anthony. I want to be the one to tell you before he does that the night I hit him, I didn't do it because he's gay and kissed me, but because he was shouting that I didn't love him and that I used him. It got to the point that not only did I hit him, I also called him a bunch of slurs." He had a look of sadness on his face as he was saying all this, and I was feeling very insecure and not sure how to handle the situation; my body was telling me to run for my life, but my mind wanted to know more.

We sat there in the quiet for what seemed like forever when my phone buzzed. It was a text from Anthony.

I can't come back. I'm sorry, I will tell you everything tomorrow. Don't listen to their lies xoxo.

I looked at the two guys sitting across from me and said, "Well, that was Anthony; he said he's not coming back, so I guess that's it for him tonight." They both sighed. I continued, "I have to ask...you said he was screaming that you didn't love him and used him; what was that all about?"

Allen looked at me as if I just shot his dog. Mark said, "Allen, he doesn't have to follow the no personal talk rule tonight; I think the ship has sailed with Anthony storming out."

Allen sighed. "We got drunk together at my place one night, and he was telling me how he was attracted to me and all that, and I didn't stop him and let it go on for a few weeks, as it was usually playful, but then he started to get more serious, and when I told him I didn't like him like that, that we're friends and I'm straight, he took it poorly, and that's how we got to the incident."

I looked at him and thought, *You're a monster to lead someone on and let them believe there's a chance when there never was one.* I then had to make sure I was correct. "So you led him on and let him think there was a chance you two would date?" I said in a tone that made it clear I wanted the honest answer and wanted it now.

Allen could tell this and said, "Yes, I did. I knew it was wrong, and I've learned what a shitty person I was. I've tried to make it up to him, but he won't answer my calls or texts. I told you that the other night when you were waiting on your...date."

There was a long pause followed by a look at Mark, then at me, then back to Mark; this went on for a few moments before Allen said, "Your date was with Anthony. It makes sense now. Alessia knew who it was but wouldn't tell Mark; both of you said you were busy, and Anthony went mad when the incident was brought up."

Mark grabbed Allen by the shoulder. "Allen, it's not our business. I know you think we have to protect David from Anthony, but we don't."

Allen looked at him with eyes of fire, the kind that looks deep into a person's soul, before agreeing. After that, we all decided not to speak of it again unless we all agreed, and we went on to discuss how the game would go next week and had a pleasant rest of our evening at the "pub."

The three of us walked back together as Mark was going over to Alessia's. Mark and I decided to take the stairs while Allen took the elevator. Once on my floor, I saw Anthony was waiting at my door. Mark just looked at me and walked off to Alessia's apartment, and once he was inside, I approached Anthony.

"Hey, I'm so sorry I ran off," he said in a sad voice.

I let him into the apartment, made us some tea, and we sat on the couch.

"So, did they tell you how I'm a monster and to stay away from me?" Anthony muttered, in a tone that gave a clear impression of *I know you talked about me after I left, and I know they lied.*

I knew there was no way out of this. "Well, Allen did tell me about how he led you on and then used slurs the night things went out of control."

Anthony looked at me in disbelief. "Led me on? Is that what they told you, that he was playing with me? He was in love with me, and I with him, but his grandfather is a southern preacher, and Allen will not accept his sexuality."

This was a shock, but I didn't know if this was true or another one of his lies. I was not looking for a fight, so I said, "Look, I don't care what happened in the past with you guys; all I know is that I think I like you, and I want to try and make us work, but I don't want any more lies, okay?"

Anthony smiled at this. "Okay. I think we can make this work, and I promise I'll make you happy." With this, he leaned in to kiss me again, and this time, I was prepared. He ended up staying the night but slept on the couch and, in the morning, was out early to miss Mark and Allen.

After he left, I sat there with a smile on my face. I was starting to be true to myself, and now I had a person in my life who could become something serious. Allen, Mark, and I had become closer because of all of this, and I felt like I could now be the true me. Today was going to be a good day, and I was ready to take on the world.

Chapter 10
GAME DAY

The following week was quiet. Mark didn't mention anything about what had happened or ask about what Anthony and I talked about when in class, and Allen was just not around, it seemed. I was busy with classes and papers I wanted to have done before the upcoming break. My phone buzzed; it was Alessia.

Can you come over? I'm freaking out and I need your advice.

I closed my laptop and let her know I would be right over. I headed out and knocked on her door. I could hear her running for the door as fast as she could before she answered.

"David, thank god, come in, please." She dragged me into her apartment with the force of what felt like a thousand people.

"Oh my god, Alessia, what's wrong?" I asked her with genuine worry that she was in trouble.

"Oh, I want your help picking an outfit for your game today. Something that'll work for both the game and the date Mark and I are going on after."

In my mind, I was like, *Seriously, this is what the big panic was? Why did I have to come right over to pick out an outfit? Do all women have their gay friends do this?* I was not fashionable, and I hoped she knew I wouldn't be great at this. We went through her whole closet, and I was very little help. She settled on a simple top with a jumper and a nice pair of jeans and trainers. For those who don't know, a jumper is a sweater and trainers are tennis shoes.

After the long event of helping Alessia get her outfit all set and complete, I had just enough time to head back to my place and get dressed. I put on my shorts and jersey, grabbed my bag, and headed out. Alessia was waiting for me in the hall to walk together to the field. Once at the field, Alessia ran over to Mark, and Anthony came running up to me. He hugged me and said he was glad to see me. I smiled and embraced him back; we did this in a way to make sure we weren't too obvious, but also, we knew our friends knew now, so we didn't have to hide as much, but with my anxiety and Anthony's, we still decided not to be completely open with our feelings for one another.

Allen came over and said, "Hey, you two, are we ready for today? David, you'll start, and Anthony will be the backup goalie."

Allen walked off, and Anthony smiled at me before saying, "Well, I was hoping to start, but now I can sit on the sidelines and watch you play. That's more fun for me anyway." He was so cute, and the fact he wanted to watch and cheer for me made me warm inside.

The game started, and it was a slow start to the match; the centers and forwards kept the ball on the other side of the field, so I didn't have to do much. I wanted them to let up some so I could show off for Anthony and impress him with my skills on the field. The ball broke loose and was heading right for me; I sprinted at full speed and sent the ball flying. The kick was so hard I sent it to the other goal, and while I didn't score from that distance, Alessia and Anthony were cheering on the sidelines. I felt great and was confident for the rest of the game. Whenever the ball crossed the center line, I was aggressive; I was having one of the best games of my life, and the man who liked me, and whom I liked back, was cheering for me. I didn't even think about my anxiety or depression.

The game ended, and we won three-two. With such a close win, the team rushed to the field, and everyone was jumping around and cheering. I was looking for Anthony, but Allen and Mark grabbed me. We jumped up and down. After it calmed down, I found Anthony, and we ran to each other and hugged. He picked me up and spun me around. "You were so great! I can't believe how great you were," he said while still spinning me. I don't know what overcame me, but once he stopped talking, I kissed him. He didn't stop me and kissed me back; everything was perfect at that moment.

Allen and Mark walked over. Mark and Alessia said their goodbyes and headed off to their date. Allen asked if we wanted to get something to eat. Anthony was hesitant, but I proposed we all go back to my place and hang out. This went over well with both of them, and we started the walk back to my place.

Once we arrived, I put on a pot of tea, and we changed out of our soccer clothes and into our regular clothes. Allen was in the bathroom changing, and Anthony and I were in my room. Anthony finished and went out to take the kettle off the heat. Allen walked out of the bathroom and into my room. I turned around to see him shirtless. His chest mesmerized me; he was well built, as mentioned before, and now his abs were right in plain view. I couldn't help but look. We headed out and sat on the couch. Anthony came over with the tea, and we chatted and talked about what we wanted to eat. We decided on a pizza, and Allen called and ordered it.

The pizza came, and the three of us attacked it as we were all starving from our game. The rest of the evening went well; we talked, laughed, and watched TV. Everything was going great, but in my mind, I could not get the sight of Allen out of my head and him standing there in my room like that in front of me. I wanted him, and I knew he was not in reach. I looked over at Anthony. He was being pleasant tonight. There was no tension between him and Allen, and he was wearing some pretty short shorts and a shirt, and it turned me on. I wanted both of them badly; I could feel it in my gut. I wished they would say, "Let's do this." My heart started to race as I thought about it.

Sitting there in my thoughts, I didn't notice Allen stand up until he spoke. "All right, guys, it's getting late. I'm going to head out."

I looked at the clock and saw it was 11:00 p.m. "Oh yeah, look at the time; let me help you get your things." After I stood up and helped him to the door, we said our goodbyes, and I shut the door behind him.

Once Allen was gone, I turned around to see Anthony standing there. "I guess I should get going," he said.

I didn't want him to leave, so I let my feelings overcome me. I grabbed him and pushed him against the wall and started kissing him passionately. He started kissing me back, and things started to get hot between us; we were grabbing and kissing each other all over. We headed to my bed and things escalated quickly. The night went on well into the early hours, and I didn't care.

The following day, I woke up before Anthony, so I got dressed, put the kettle on, and started making breakfast. Anthony walked out of the room in his underwear. "Good morning," he said with a yawn.

"Good morning," I said. "Breakfast is almost ready; you should put some clothes on."

He looked at me. "Really, after the night we just had? Do you want me to put some pants on?" He stood up and returned to the room; a few moments later, he returned with pants but still no shirt. Anthony was built as well, not as much as Allen, but he was still lovely to look at, so I didn't mind him not wearing a shirt, and after last night, I didn't care if he was clothed. We had our breakfast and talked about what it meant last night; I felt I needed validation that what we had done was more than just a hookup.

After breakfast, Anthony and I had another round of fun like our night prior. We showered and dressed, and Anthony collected his things to head out. At the door, we chatted some more, and before he left, he said, "I really had fun last night, and not just because of what happened with us, but even with Allen. It's been forever since things went so well, and I would like to do it again."

I wanted for it to happen again but I also wanted it to mean more. I looked at him and said, I would like that but I want more than a random hookup when it feels right between us." Anthony looked at me but didn't say anything. I said, "I mean, we don't have to put a label on it, but maybe we can be more official as people who are more than friends."

Anthony smiled and then spoke. "I think we should be more official too, and maybe we can be boyfriends one day, but maybe we should have another date first."

I happily agreed to this, and he walked off. I shut the door and smiled to myself; things were getting better and I hadn't had a panic attack from this, which was a step in the right direction. I sat at my desk and started working on my schoolwork for class the following day.

Chapter 11
UPCOMING BREAK

Our break was coming up next week, and everyone was making plans. I was confused as we don't have Thanksgiving in Scotland, and while most people were going home for the week, Anthony included, I was still trying to figure out what to do. I called Sam to check in with her and see how things were going. When she answered, her voice was so excited to hear from me, and we talked for hours about life. I told her about me and Anthony, how things were getting more serious, and what I should do with my time on the break, though I didn't want to fly home for a week. Sam was helpful, and even though she wanted me to come home she agreed it was silly. We said our goodbyes, and I got ready for my classes for the day. I grabbed my bag and headed for school.

Once in class, Mark, as usual, sat next to me. We chatted, waiting for the small professor to finish talking so we could take our exam. He was telling me how he was taking Alessia home to meet his parents and how excited he was to finally bring home someone he felt his parents would approve of. I explained how I had no idea what to do as Thanksgiving made no sense to me as I had never celebrated it. Mark didn't have any advice for me and said to ask Allen as he didn't think he was going anywhere either and maybe we could have Friendsgiving. I wasn't sure what Friendsgiving was, but after talking with Mark some more, I learned it was like Thanksgiving, but instead of going to see family, you spend it with friends. I didn't need an excuse to see Allen and looked forward to asking him after class today.

Once class was over, I pulled out my phone and texted him. *Do you want to get lunch today? I have something to ask you.*

Allen responded almost immediately, like he was waiting for someone to contact him.

Lunch sounds great. Meet me in the dining hall on campus in 15 minutes.

I headed for the dining hall. Once I arrived, I found Allen sitting at a table on his laptop. I walked to him, and as I approached, he closed his computer, smiled, and spoke. "David, I'm so glad you wanted to have lunch. What are you in the mood for? My treat." We ended up getting sandwiches, nothing fancy, but I was okay with that. Once we sat down, Allen asked, "So what did you want to ask me?"

"Oh, well, Mark said you were staying in town as well for Thanksgiving and thought maybe you and I could do a Friendsgiving."

Allen gave me a smile, then frowned. "I would love to do a Friendsgiving with you, but I'm going out of town. I was looking at plane tickets when you came up. I'm going to London to see my aunt."

I frowned but understood and said, "Oh, it's fine. I thought I would ask, but I'll figure something else out if you have plans."

Allen looked at me with an odd expression on his face, and then out of nowhere, he said, "I have a great idea. Come with me."

I looked at him in confusion. "What?" I said.

"I mean it. My aunt would love you, and we can even travel to Scotland and see your family while there. It'll be a blast."

I hadn't been planning on going home, but a trip to London and then my hometown with Allen could be fun. "Yeah, I guess that can be arranged. I'll let my parents know we'll be coming."

Allen could not hold in his excitement. We planned the trip and headed on our way.

Once at home, I texted Sam to let her know I was coming home for a few days after all, and once I was in Scotland, I would contact her, and we could catch up. Then I called my mum. The phone only rang once before I heard Mum's voice. "David, hi, how are you? Dad and I miss you. Are you okay? Granddad and Grandma were here last night, and we all said we wished you would come home on your next break."

I smiled, knowing I was about to make her day. "Well, that's why I'm calling. I'm going with a friend to London for a few days over the break, and we plan to spend a few days of our trip at home."

Mum went into a frenzy. I heard, "Franco, David's coming home, and he's bringing a friend! We have so much to do to get ready for them."

I smiled as Dad tried to calm her and explain that it was just a visit and not a big deal. Mum and I hammered out what days I would be there and when I would be heading back to America before she had to go to get things ready and tell my grandparents.

Later on in the day, I met with Anthony. I wanted to tell him my plans, as we agreed not to hide or lie to each other and had both been very good about it. When he came over for dinner, we had a pleasant conversation about him going home. He was sorry I couldn't come, but now wasn't a good time, and he hoped I would find something to do.

This gave me the opening I was looking for. "Well..." I nervously said, "I've made plans and want you to know them so you're not surprised when we return from break." Anthony looked at me intently, waiting for me to continue. "Allen and I are going to go to London to see his aunt and then spend a few days in my village to see my family."

He looked as if he was about to explode. "Oh, you and Allen are taking a trip together?" he said in a tone that showed he was not happy at all.

I spoke calmly and firmly. "Well, you're going home, and I can't go with you; Mark and Alessia are going to see his family. I was going to stay here, but Allen wanted a travel companion, and this gives me a chance to visit home. I would have taken you, but you're set on seeing your family."

He looked even more furious now. I was sitting there waiting for the fight that was about to ensue. He went to speak but closed his mouth; I just kept sitting there. My anxiety was rising by the second, and I felt a panic attack coming on. I'd known this would be a touchy subject, but I didn't want to lie to him.

I started to get dizzy and felt like I would pass out from the situation. Just then, Anthony began to talk again. "You know, I'm glad that you were honest with me, but I don't want you going on a vacation with Allen. I'm not comfortable with it, and if you insist on going, then I'm going to see an old friend when I'm back home."

I was dumbfounded; how could he tell me I couldn't travel with a friend? Plus, why would I care if he saw people when he was back home? I was sure this old friend was an ex, but I didn't care if he saw them; if they stayed friends, why should I mind? I felt myself changing from being nervous to getting upset. Why was he trying to hurt me like this? I felt that I might regret this, but I had to confront him and tell him I was going, and that was that.

I started to open my mouth, but before I could talk, Anthony interrupted. "You know what, I don't care; enjoy your trip." With that, he stood up from the table and walked out the door. I just sat there. I had no idea what his issue was, but now I felt more down on myself and insecure than I had since moving to America.

I texted Allen and Alessia, asking them both to come over, as I really needed to talk and was feeling down and heading to a dark place in my mind. They both responded they would be right over. A few minutes later, there was knocking on my door. I answered, and Alessia grabbed me and pulled me in for a hug—one of those hugs where you feel like you're in a vise grip, and there was no way out but to accept it. After she let go, I let them in, put the kettle on to make a fresh pot of tea, and we all sat on the couch.

"So what's going on?" Alessia asked.

I filled them in on my and Anthony's fight, and how he stormed out in the middle of it. I went on to tell them how this made me feel so unimportant to him, and I wasn't sure why he was so against me being friends with Allen and us traveling together. Allen just sat there while Alessia tried to devise a logical reason why he might be upset. I continued and filled them in on how he wanted to upset me by saying if I went on this trip, he would meet up with an old friend I assumed was an ex.

Allen, at this moment, chimed in. "Well, it's clear he's still upset about the incident, but I don't think that should stop you from seeing your family on this trip. Anthony will get over it, and him trying to hurt you is shitty, and you shouldn't allow that to happen."

I knew he was right, but with my self-esteem already being so low and this being the first relationship I had ever been in, I didn't want to make things complicated just because I wanted to go on a vacation with a friend. I would love to take Anthony on a trip like this, but he didn't want to go; he wanted to see his family and didn't want me around. I wanted to be with him, but these things made me feel bad about myself.

We all chatted for a while about our plans: mine and Allen's trip, and Alessia and her trip with Mark. This helped me keep my mind off things, if only for the time being. We ordered takeout and just ate and talked about the things we wanted to do, and the places we wanted to see, and promised to contact each other nightly to let the others know we were safe and having fun. Alessia helped me pack some of the things I would need, and then we went to her place to do the same and finally to Allen's. After everyone was packed, Alessia and I said our goodbyes to Allen and headed back down to our apartments. Once on our floor, Alessia hugged me and promised things would get better and to give it time with Anthony. I returned to my apartment and tried to call Anthony; it rang once and went straight to voicemail. I was still feeling depressed about the situation and decided it would be for the best to just go to bed and figure it out in the morning.

The following day, when I woke up, there was a text from Anthony.

I'm sorry about last night. I was out of line, and I overreacted. If you want to go on this trip, I can't stop you, but I don't want you to go with Allen. I don't like him, and you know this, but you insist on hanging out with him, which makes me unhappy sometimes. Xoxo.

I could not believe him; in the same message, he managed to apologize for his actions and still made me feel bad at the same time. I did not respond; I didn't know how to. I was feeling worse and worse, and I just wanted to lie in my bed all day and not move; there was no motivation in me. Usually, when I get like this, I make myself get up, but not today. I allowed my depression to win and did not move.

Later in the day, there was a knock on my door. I knew I had to get up and answer it, but I still did not want to move; I just sat there listening to the knocking. This went on for minutes before my phone started to ring. I looked over and saw it was Alessia.

"Hello," I answered.

"Oh, David, I knocked on your door, but you didn't answer. I wanted to make sure you're all right after last night?"

I sighed as I was in no mood to talk, so I lied. "Yeah, I'm fine. Sorry, I was in the shower and didn't hear you knocking. I'm just getting ready for my travels tomorrow, but I promise I'll come down and see you off in a minute."

This seemed to satisfy her. We chatted for a few more minutes before hanging up so I could get ready to come down in a little while to see her and Mark off on their trip.

Half an hour later, Mark, Allen, Alessia, and I were all in the apartment complex's lobby. Mark was talking about the drive and the route he had planned to show Alessia parts of Michigan, and Allen was complaining that our flight was longer than he'd expected and he was not looking forward to it. Alessia and I were talking about how exciting it was she was going to get to see more of America even if it was still just Michigan, how excited I must be to go home and see my family, and how she missed hers. We all said our goodbyes and gave hugs as they needed to get on the road, and Allen and I helped with their luggage. We watched as the car drove off. Once out of sight, Allen and I walked back into the building and went to our apartments to ensure we had everything we needed for our trip. I hoped to hear from Anthony before he left to see his parents today, but he did not return my calls or texts, which made me feel down. Was he this upset over my travel plans? Or maybe he was busy and would call me when he arrived tonight. I hoped so. Once back in my apartment, my depression started to take hold, and I crawled back into my bed and broke down before drifting off to sleep.

Chapter 12
FLIGHT

The morning had come, and it was the day of our flight. Still feeling very down about Anthony so I wasn't in as happy of a mood as I should have been, even though I was about to travel to Europe with a good friend and someone I fancied, and soon I would see my family and Sam again. With our flight later in the day, I spent most of it double and triple checking that I had not forgotten anything and that I would have everything I needed for the holiday: enough clothes, extra jumpers just in case, etc. Once I was confident that Mum would not be able to say I didn't pack properly, I reached for my phone to text Anthony.

Hope you made it safe. I miss you and cannot wait to see you when we return from our trip.

I then texted Allen to check he was ready and that he had double-checked to make sure he had everything he would need.

There was still plenty of time before we needed to head to the airport, but I'm a planner. With my anxiety, I hate for surprises or something to come up that I could have foreseen and fixed beforehand, so I went online to check if the plane was still on time and to see if I could check us in yet. Once in the system, I could see everything was showing on time. I was able to check us in, and while doing so, I noticed there were two seats in business class next to each other that were open. I remembered Allen complaining to Mark the day before that the flight was longer than he expected and thought this would be a pleasant surprise for him. I upgraded our seats, paid the difference, and printed our boarding passes. I looked at my phone to see if either of them had texted me back and saw there was a text from Anthony.

Made it fine, having a blast. Text me when your plane lands.

This was cold compared to his standard texts to me, but at least I knew he was okay, and the fact that he wanted me to text him once the plane landed made me feel like he still cared. Still, I was feeling sad about how things were between us and hoped I would feel better once I saw my family.

The time had come for us to depart for the airport. I grabbed my bags and the boarding passes and headed to the lobby to wait for Allen. Once down, I double-checked my phone to see if Anthony had texted me, but there was nothing. Then I called and double-checked that the car Allen had ordered was on the way. A few moments later, Allen came into the lobby from the elevator. He had the same look of excitement on his face as a child come Christmas morning. You could tell he was looking forward to this trip and he didn't even know about the surprise of upgraded seats; I decided to keep this a secret until we started boarding the plane. The car pulled up to the front of the building, and we loaded our bags into the boot, what Americans call the trunk, and headed to the airport.

The whole ride there, Allen talked about how excited he was to see his aunt and the UK, which he had always wanted to visit but it had never happened. Now he was on his way to see his favorite family member, he said, and he was going with one of his good friends and was even getting to see where he was from. I just smiled. To me, this didn't seem like a big deal. I was going home, but then I thought about my excitement to come to America for college; this was the same for Allen. He was going somewhere new and exciting, just like I did, and that made me understand his excitement for this trip. Plus, he was getting to see family. Coming from a close-knit family, I knew what it was like to be excited to see them, so I stayed quiet and allowed him to ramble about how this would be the best trip ever.

Once we arrived at the airport and collected our luggage, we headed for the check-in lines. The airport was just as busy as the day we arrived for my move-in, with people going in all directions to make their flights to see family for Thanksgiving. Allen and I got in line and slowly worked our way to the front. The agent was an older woman with a sweet voice. When it was our turn, she said, "Hello, dears, traveling home to see the parents for the holiday, are we?"

Allen, not being able to contain his excitement, blurted out, "Oh, no, we're friends going to see my aunt in London, then we're heading to Scotland to his home village to see his family."

The old woman smiled before saying, "How lovely it is to see friends willing to give up their holiday to spend it together in a different country."

She sent our bags down the conveyor belt, and we headed for security. The security line was moving even slower than the check-in desk, and the agent running it was short with everyone. I was starting to feel anxious and just wanted to get it done. When it came to our turn, Allen went first with no problem; however, when it was my turn to step into the X-ray machine, it malfunctioned, and I had to stand there while they fixed it. Each moment that passed, I was getting more and more overwhelmed. I could feel my heart racing, and I wanted to run for it. Finally, the machine started to work, and the agent said I was all set. I dashed out, collected my things, and met with Allen to head for our gate.

Once we found our gate and got settled, I needed to find something to eat. Luckily, our plane wasn't leaving for another hour, and a few restaurants were nearby. Allen didn't want anything, so I went exploring alone. While walking, my phone buzzed; it was a text from Anthony.

Have you left yet?

What a weird question, I thought. He knew when my flight was. I texted it to him earlier today so he would know and be able to track it. Did he forget? Was there some other reason he wanted to know? Whatever the reason was, I was just glad to hear from him.

I responded, *Not yet, the plane takes off in an hour. I'm walking around the airport alone, looking for something to eat.*

During this, I found a sandwich shop and figured it would be the fastest option. While ordering, my phone buzzed again.

Why isn't Allen with you? Did he do something?

This annoyed me; he was mad when I was with Allen *and* when I wasn't. Was he trying to start a fight? I finished my order and waited for it before I texted him back.

Everything's fine. I just wanted something to eat, and he didn't; we don't have to be right next to each other the entire trip, do we? This way, he can do whatever he wants, and I can talk with you.

His questioning irritated me, and I was starting to wonder if this trip was a bad idea; how would I enjoy myself when Anthony was questioning my every move and I was worrying about him getting upset? He was the one who hadn't wanted to spend the break together, not me. He didn't respond the entire time I was eating my food, and once I was cleaned up, I texted him to let him know I was heading back to the gate and would be turning my phone off until the plane was in the air and would let him know when we were approaching London.

Back at the gate, I found Allen sitting in a corner on his phone; not wanting to disturb whatever he was doing, I sat down, pulled a schoolbook out of my bag, and started reading it.

Allen noticed this. "Did you bring schoolwork on our vacation? Man, what is wrong with you?" he said playfully.

"Well, I did. We'll be on the plane for some time, and I'm sure we'll get sick of each other at some point."

He just looked at me, then said, "There are two problems with your theory. First, I don't think I'll get bored of you or this trip; secondly, I need to teach you how to live a little. Luckily for you, my aunt is a blast."

I just laughed. "Well, you can teach me to live a little, and in exchange, when we get to my village, I'll show you what real work is by taking you to the farm."

I was feeling smug; I knew a day on the farm would make him regret his choices, but of course, Allen, not wanting to be outshined, just said, "I'll take your bet, and when I run circles around you on your farm you're gonna wish you didn't make that comment."

We laughed, then I returned to my book and Allen to his phone while we waited for boarding to start.

A few minutes later, the desk agent made the announcement over the PA. "Now boarding our guests who need extra time and our first-class passengers."

Allen leaned over to me and whispered, "Should we act like we need extra time since our boarding is towards the end?"

I smiled, and I figured this was too much fun with him not knowing and suggested that when business class started boarding, we get in that line and see if they notice. Allen was all for this when we heard over the PA, "Now boarding our business-class passengers."

We stood up and headed to the line. I pulled out our boarding passes and handed them to the check-in attendant; she scanned them and handed them back, then said, "Welcome to business class, enjoy your flight, and thank you for flying with Air Canada." As we started walking down the breeze, Allen was saying he couldn't believe it worked and that it must have been a glitch in the system. At this point, I knew it was time to let him in on what I had done, so I said to him as I handed him the tickets, "Tell me what row and seat numbers we have. I don't remember."

Allen took the tickets from my hand and started reading them. After a moment, he said, "This must be a mistake. These tickets say row ten, seats one and two, but those are business class seats; we didn't book these."

I smiled. "Well, I wanted to surprise you. When I checked the site this morning, I saw the seats and knew you were having issues with how long of a flight this was, so I upgraded them."

Allen looked at me with the biggest grin I had ever seen before saying, "I could kiss you right now. This is so amazing. I don't know how to make this up to you, but I will somehow, I promise."

Well, a kiss from you would make it better, I thought, but alas, this would never happen. We found our seats and got settled while we waited for the rest of the plane to load and prepare for the pushback onto the runway.

The plane was soon loaded, and we started to push back. I was now less stressed and worried about what was going on with Anthony and was looking forward to being home and spending time with Allen. We were sitting on the runway waiting for our turn to take off when Allen leaned over to me and said, "Oh, I forgot to tell you, but I have a fear of flying. Once we're in the air I'm fine for the most part, but do you mind if I hold your hand?"

Who was I to say no? I put out my hand for him, and he grabbed it firmly as the plane started to pick up speed and whiz faster and faster, and with each moment, Allen was squeezing harder and harder. Soon we were in the air. Once the plane leveled out, Allen started to loosen his grip, but I didn't want it to end, so I squeezed back, and Allen took the hint that I wasn't ready to let go. We held hands until the crew started coming around with the beverage service. I was sad to let go of his hand, and I knew I would not get this chance again until we had to head home, but I didn't want to make it awkward.

After food and drinks, Allen decided to get some sleep. I was too excited about how things were going so I wasn't tired. I pulled my book out of my bag and kept reading. I would glance over occasionally to check on Allen. He looked so cute sitting there, and I wanted to lean over and cuddle him, but how would he react? Would it be another situation like with him and Anthony? What if Anthony were to find out? He was already very on edge lately, and I wouldn't want to create more issues between him and Allen. This made me feel down. I liked Anthony and wanted to be with him, but I also wanted Allen, and he was so close yet so far. I figured this was a good time to text Anthony.

On the plane, should be landing in about seven hours. I miss you and hope you're okay.

Anthony texted back within seconds. *Glad you're safe. Let me know when you land. Be safe, and let me know if Allen gives you any trouble.*

I was happy that he wanted to make sure I was safe, but again, what was with the Allen obsession? I had never given him a reason not to trust Allen and me or to think I would ever be in danger around him. I always felt awful when Anthony would say bad things about Allen, and not just because I liked him; I wanted all of us to get along, and I wanted everyone to be friends.

I decided to get some sleep. With our flight leaving America at 6:00 p.m., it would be 6:30 a.m. when we landed in London. I put my phone and books away and settled down on my bed to get some rest, but no matter how much I tried, I couldn't bring myself to get any rest, I looked over at Allen; he was fast asleep without a care in the world. How cute he looked sleeping there. I wanted to cuddle up next to him to see if that would help me, but I was too scared. I finally closed my eyes and hoped to fall asleep. Sometime later, I woke to turbulence; Allen was sitting in his seat with a severe look of panic on his face. I reached out my hand for him, and he grabbed it instantly. I smiled and saw that he was starting to relax. I was overjoyed to have his hand in mine again, and we sat there looking at one another. Once the turbulence died, I drifted back to sleep, still holding Allen's hand. It was a perfect moment.

I woke around 5:00 a.m. Allen was already awake. "Hey, you, I ordered us breakfast; the steward should be bringing it momentarily."

I smiled; how sweet of him to order for me. I wondered if Anthony would have done the same. The more I let my mind linger on it, the more I decided he wouldn't have. He could be so self-centered sometimes, but his texts since I left had been more caring, so maybe I was wrong. The steward brought over our breakfast. It was a proper English breakfast: bacon, poached eggs, sausage, and toast with a fried tomato. I was happy to see it; this meant I was getting closer to being home. Allen had never seen an English breakfast and was surprised by it. I laughed, we ate our breakfast, and by the time it was all cleaned up, we started our descent into London. Allen was getting excited, which was making me anxious; while I was excited about this trip, I felt the pressure of meeting his aunt and spending more time with him.

We were both waiting for the bounce as the plane touched down, and as we came closer and closer to the ground, Allen started to show signs of fear again. I reached out my hand for him, and he smiled as he grabbed it. A few seconds later, we touched down, and people in the plane started to clap. This always drove me crazy; why were they clapping? Allen released his grip. The captain's voice came over the PA. "Hello everyone, welcome to London. The weather is a fabulous five degrees."

Allen gave a look like he had not been preparing for such cold weather, I explained while trying my hardest not to laugh at the confused expression on his face. "It's Celsius; for you, it would be forty-one degrees."

He laughed before saying, "I was worried there for a minute; I brought clothes for cold weather, but not that cold."

We laughed as we waited for the plane to taxi to the terminal.

Once the plane pulled into the terminal, Allen and I stood up to head for the exit before the mad dash of people started coming down the aisle. Once off the plane, we headed for baggage claim. While we waited for our bags, this high-pitched voice came from behind us. "Allen, darling, I'm so glad to see you."

We both turned around to see an older woman standing there. Allen smiled and hugged her. "Aunt Vi, I'm so glad to see you. This is my friend David I was telling you about."

Aunt Vi looked at me, put her arms out for a hug, and said, "Hello, darling, I am so excited to meet you. Come give me a hug."

I hugged her. "It's so nice to meet you. Allen has been so excited for us to see you here."

Aunt Vi looked at me, then at Allen. "Really, you were excited to see me? I feel so special. No one ever comes to see me in England, and I see the family for big events when I travel to America."

Allen smiled. "Of course I was excited. You're my favorite person in the world, and I wish we could see each other more."

Aunt Vi smiled. At this moment, the conveyor started, and bags began to come down. Allen and I collected our luggage, and Aunt Vi led us out of the airport to hail a cab. Once in the cab, we drove through the twisted and turns of the London streets before pulling up to a charming semi-detached home with a garden in the back of a sunroom. We went inside, and Aunt Vi showed us the bedroom we would share during our stay. We got settled and headed down to find Aunt Vi making a pot of tea.

We talked for hours about the trip, what Allen had been up to, how the school year had been going, and what was new with the family. Aunt Vi was also interested in me and how someone from Scotland was doing in America, and how Allen and I became friends. Everything was going great, but I forgot to text Anthony because of all the excitement and travel. I only remembered when my phone buzzed.

Did you make it? Your plane should have landed hours ago.

I freaked out inside. Oh crap, I forgot I hadn't texted him back.

I am so sorry. I meant to text you. Allen's aunt picked us up at the airport and made us tea when we arrived. I completely forgot. I'm safe and hope you're having a good time with your family.

His response was short, as expected. All I got was, *Okay, family is good.* That was it. I felt sick and terrible that I had forgotten; now he was mad at me. I didn't mean to forget. Allen's aunt had been a blast, and I'd lost track of time. I started to feel down, but I put on a brave face and returned to my conversation with Allen and Aunt Vi.

Chapter 13
VACATION IN LONDON

We spent the first day with Aunt Vi, talking, laughing, and having a great time. For lunch, Aunt Vi made us sandwiches and lemonade, and we ate out in the garden, followed by a pot of tea. Later, we walked down to the shops at the end of the street and did some window shopping, and for dinner, Aunt Vi took us out to a nice upscale restaurant in town. Everything was terrific, and I was enjoying myself. However, I couldn't get over Anthony being upset; I still felt down and didn't know how to handle it. After dinner, we walked back to the house, and I excused myself and crawled into bed. Allen came up and asked if I was okay.

I responded, "I'm well, just tired. I guess it's the jet lag."

Allen smiled. "Well, Aunt Vi and I will be sitting in the parlor if you change your mind." He closed the door and went back down the stairs. I felt horrible, like the other day when I didn't want to move or leave my bed. I could hear Aunt Vi and Allen downstairs, and I wanted to join them but couldn't move. I was utterly paralyzed with depression.

Later that night, Allen came into the bedroom, trying to be quiet so as not to wake me; he was not doing an excellent job at it, but I made it seem like I was still sleeping. I watched as he changed into his pajamas and crawled into bed. Having him beside me felt nice. The bed was only full size, so we had to sleep right next to each other. Feeling his body against mine made me come out of my depression; why did this seem right to me? I knew there would never be anything between us, but this calmed me more than any time I had been next to Anthony. I decided to be daring. I moved closer, and he put his arm around me. Words could not express how excited this made me. I was now close to Allen in a way I never thought possible, and I fell asleep with a big smile.

Early the following day, I made sure I was up before Allen so as not to cause an issue; I did not want anything to go wrong. I put on a jumper as it was very chilly this morning and found Aunt Vi in the kitchen. "Oh, good morning, Vi, how are you? Can I help with anything?"

I must have startled her as she jumped and turned around. "Oh, darling, you scared me. I'm not used to having company, and when I heard a man's voice, I was confused. I'm all right, dear, the kettle is on, and the tea should be ready soon. Has Allen woken yet?"

I smiled. "Not yet; he was sleeping soundly when I left the room."

Aunt Vi laughed. "Yes, he was always a late sleeper, ever since he was a little boy." She looked into the distance briefly before saying, "So Allen tells me that you're having relationship troubles."

This took me aback. "He told you that?" I asked, surprised.

"Oh dear, I didn't mean to pry; I always wished Allen would find someone right for him. I never married or had children, and Allen is the closest thing I have to a child; we talk about everything. He cares for you, or he wouldn't have told me about you or brought you here."

Inside, I was warmed by this, but I didn't want to tell Allen's aunt that I fancied him. "Well, my boyfriend has an issue with me coming on this trip," I said sadly.

"Oh? And why is that?" Aunt Vi asked, her tone sincere.

"Well, he and Allen had an altercation before I met them, and it's strained their relationship ever since, and I think he's afraid that Allen will be mean to me."

Aunt Vi looked confused before she asked, "Do you mean the kiss?"

I was shocked that she knew of it. "Oh well, I didn't know you knew about that, but yeah, I guess Anthony is worried Allen will hit me too as he did him."

Aunt Vi sighed. "Well, darling, there are things about Allen that you still don't know, and I don't know if I'm the one to tell you about them." At this point, we could hear Allen coming down the stairs. Aunt Vi and I got up from the table and made fresh cups of tea while Aunt Vi finished breakfast.

During breakfast, Aunt Vi talked about Allen when he was a child and some of the embarrassing things he did. Allen was turning very red from this, and I was having the time of my life. Then the conversation turned to what we planned to do for the day. I wanted to go to the Tower of London and the Victoria and Albert Museum, and Allen wanted to check out Borough Market. Aunt Vi thought these were all grand ideas. She said we should start at the market and then go to the tower, and then if there was time to go to the museum and if not, there was always tomorrow. We agreed, finished breakfast, and went upstairs to prepare for the day. Allen had no shame and was comfortable around me. As soon as we were in the room, he stripped down to nothing but his underwear. I tried not to stare and focused on getting ready. Once the two of us had finished getting ready we headed downstairs to hail a cab and head off to the market.

The market was busy when we arrived, and there was so much to see; in every direction we looked, there were stalls selling food from all different corners of the world. Allen was holding my hand and dragging me from one place to the other to avoid losing me in the mass of people. We were having a blast. Allen finally took a break from running around, and I took this break as a chance to text Anthony.

Doing some sightseeing. I hope you're having a good day. I can't wait to tell you all about it.

Anthony opened the message but did not respond; I figured he was busy and didn't think much about it. Allen came up to me with some food and drinks. We found a nearby park to eat and headed off to see the Tower of London. Since it was not that far, we decided it was best to walk.

Once at the tower, we got into the queue to get our tickets. Allen was looking all around in awe at the sights and sounds of London, and I was watching him, thinking he was so cute. I loved how much of a great time he was having, and I hoped my village would be as exciting to him as London had been. We reached the front of the queue, and I ordered our tickets from the attendant. She looked at me and gave a sweet smile "Oh, your accent. Are you from Scotland, dear?"

I laughed on the inside "Yes, I am. My mate and I are here on holiday from America."

She gave me one more sweet look as she handed me our tickets. "Well, welcome to the Tower of London, and welcome to the UK to your mate."

We headed to the gate and started to explore. We were having a great time when Allen's phone rang. He answered and walked off for a minute. I took this chance to try calling Anthony; the phone rang, and I heard his voicemail. "Hey Anthony, I just wanted to call and see how you're doing. I miss you and can't wait to see you." Allen walked back over, and we continued our exploration of the tower. The day was still young, so we decided to go somewhere else and keep the museum for tomorrow so we could have plenty of time without feeling rushed. We decided to walk over to the Sky Garden.

The Sky Garden was unique and romantic, with so many different plants and trees from around the world, and the sight of the skyline was breathtaking. Allen and I sat there for some time, taking it all in. I leaned my head on his shoulder as we watched the sun start to go down. He did not stop me; it was one of those romantic moments when two platonic friends could share something special. I was getting hungry, and we decided to have supper at Larch. I was looking forward to some Italian but had yet to have any decent Italian since moving to America. Dad used to take two days off a month to cook traditional dishes from Italy for supper, and it was always the best.

We were having a pleasant dinner when I told Allen, "So Aunt Vi told me that you were concerned with mine and Anthony's relationship." He just stared at me, so I said, "I'm not mad that you're worried; I'm just curious what concerns you."

Allen sighed. "Well, I've noticed you've been more anxious and depressed lately, and I assumed it has something to do with your relationship. Also, why did he not take you with him to see his family? After the whole mess of not telling people you two were on a date, now he doesn't want to take you home for a holiday?"

Everything he said made sense, but I kept thinking there had to be a valid reason. I made an excuse. "Well, we aren't there yet in our relationship. I'm sure he'll tell his parents about me while there, and I'll meet them the next holiday."

Allen frowned. "I don't want to talk about this right now," he said in a hurt tone.

I didn't want to push the issue so I changed the subject.

After dinner, we continued walking around the garden. Allen finally spoke. "I'm worried about you, David. I know what Anthony is like, and I just don't want to see you hurt." He went to say something else, but at that moment, my phone rang. I looked at it. "Oh, it's Anthony; I should take this." I walked off before Allen could say anything and answered. "Hey babe, how are you?"

Anthony spoke in a severe tone. "Hey, how are things? Has Allen been nice to you? What have you two done all day? Things have been busy here. That's why I didn't text back."

He was bombarding me, and I was annoyed that my question was pretty much overlooked. I answered his questions and took his short responses, and then I asked him, "So why did you not take me to meet your family?"

I could hear Anthony breathing harder before he went into a rant. "Why are you so mad that I didn't ask you to come with me? It's not a big deal, David, seriously."

I started feeling bad about myself again. "You're right, it's not. I'm sorry I said that. I'll talk to you tomorrow. Allen and I are about to return to his aunt's place."

With that, Anthony hung up and I headed back over to Allen. I tried to hide my sadness from him, but he saw right through it.

"Are you all right?" he asked with concern.

"Yeah, I'm fine; talking to Anthony made me realize I miss him."

Allen just looked at me, held out his hand, and suggested we should head down and hail a cab to return to his aunt's. I reached out and took his hand in mine, and we headed down to the street. Once in the cab, I sat there looking out the window as the cars passed by, still feeling down about myself after talking to Anthony, and I was wondering what Allen was going to say when he was interrupted, so I looked at him. "So what were you going to say before Anthony called?"

Allen looked at me. "Oh, I don't remember, so it wasn't important."

I figured that must have been true as he showed no signs of being deceitful. Once back at his aunt's, we headed in and went straight up to the bedroom. We both stripped down to our underwear, and I climbed into bed without putting anything on as it was warm in the room. Allen looked at me before following suit. I dozed off to sleep and felt Allen's arm wrapped around me again like the night before.

The following morning, I had awoken to find Allen was out of the room. I put on some clothes and headed down to the kitchen. There was a note. *Boys, I had to run out early this morning. I left something to eat in the fridge, Aunt Vi.* There was no sign of Allen. I looked out into the empty garden and saw the parlor was also open; he must have gone out for a walk or something, I thought. I headed back upstairs to prepare for the day, and when I walked into the room, there was Allen in nothing. I quickly shielded my eyes and apologized.

Allen just laughed. "You all right? I should have kept the towel on until I knew it was clear," he said in a joking voice.

I gave a fake laugh to hide my feelings. "Well, I was just downstairs. Your aunt had to go out but said there was food in the fridge. I'll go get showered, then I'll meet you down there."

Allen finished getting dressed and went off to the kitchen while I made my way to the bathroom.

While sitting in the shower, I could not stop thinking about walking in on Allen with nothing on. The thought of it made me hot, and I had to take care of myself before I was finished. Once I was dried and dressed, I headed downstairs to find Allen trying to figure out the kettle. Aunt Vi had an old-school one that you had to heat on the stove and wait for the whistle; it's not complicated, but the one I used in America was electric and had a plate and switch. I think Allen was looking for that.

"Are you managing, Allen?" I asked as I walked into the kitchen.

"I can't find the plate that this goes on like the one in your apartment."

I laughed, and Allen looked at me like *what's so funny?* "It goes on the stove," I said, grabbing it from his hand and taking it over to the stove to start warming up. Allen looked at me, embarrassed. "Well, now that we've learned how to properly set a kettle on the stove, how about we heat up what Aunt Vi left for us?" I said in a joking but smug manner. Allen went to the fridge, pulled out the sausages and eggs Aunt Vi cooked for us before she left, and warmed them up. Once the kettle started to whistle, I took it from the stove and made us some tea while Allen plated our breakfast. We ate and chatted about what we wanted to do today if the museum was a complete waste and we ended up being bored, I didn't think a museum could be boring, but Allen seemed to doubt anything about history could be fun in any way, shape, or form. I reminded him how much he enjoyed the market and Tower of London, which are considered historic.

Both of us sat eating in silence for a moment before I asked, "So, where's your aunt? What could she have to do so early in the morning?"

Allen looked up from his plate with a smile. "Oh, well, it's a surprise we have planned for you tonight. Since we leave tomorrow, you'll have to wait."

I wouldn't say I liked surprises, especially ones for me; I hated, even more, knowing about it and not knowing what it was. I just smiled and finished my breakfast. We cleaned the kitchen and grabbed our jumpers to head out for the museum; a cab was already waiting outside. I found this odd, but Allen just got in, and we headed off. I was still amazed at how different London was compared to home and how less than a day's trip separated us. How could this city be so populated and bustling? Mine was a quiet village where everyone knew everyone, and things went slower.

We arrived at the museum, and I was getting excited. I decided to send a photo to Anthony to show him what we were doing that morning. I took the picture and sent it, not thinking anything of it.

Then he texted back, *Why are you sending me a pic of you and Allen? Are you trying to make me mad?*

I was confused. I didn't take a photo of Allen and me; I sent him a picture of me in front of the museum. I looked at the image I had taken. Allen was standing in the background, waiting for me, but he wasn't in the picture, in my opinion. I sighed, put my phone away as I didn't want a fight, and made my way into the museum with Allen.

It was quiet inside; it felt romantic. We walked around admiring the artwork and the statues, and I was having a perfect time seeing the history. The stories being told were amazing. I was still feeling down about Anthony being mad about a silly picture, but I also felt passion for the art on display. I saw Allen sitting on a bench, staring intently at the painting before him. It was of a beautiful countryside in Northern Ireland. There were no words exchanged; we just sat there. Allen then reached out his hand, still not saying anything. I took it in mine, and we kept looking at the painting. Some time had passed, about ten or fifteen minutes, when Allen started to speak. "This painting, I don't know what it is about it, but it speaks to me. I feel at peace looking at it. I know that seems odd, but it's true."

I smiled. "Well, that's the great thing about art; it makes us feel things we didn't know possible."

Allen looked at me. "This painting means more to me than a feeling. It makes me believe that I'm living a lie and should be someone completely different from who I am."

I leaned my head on his shoulder as he looked back at it. "Well, we all have our struggles in life, and we all have to find the right path."

Allen took a deep breath, and we stared at the painting a little longer before we moved on to the rest of the museum.

Allen looked at his watch. "Oh my, how time has passed; we have to go back to Aunt Vi's and get changed for your surprise."

I was bummed, I wanted to stay, but I also knew this was important to Allen, so we headed off, hailed a cab, and returned to get ready. When we arrived at the house, there was another cab there and Aunt Vi was waiting at the door. She was dressed in an exquisite gown, and when she saw us, she said, "Oh, darlings, there you are. I was wondering if you were going to make it back in time. I'll let the driver know it will just be a few minutes. Go get ready—I'll meet you in the cab."

Allen and I rushed upstairs. He opened the closet and pulled out two tuxes.

"What's going on?" I asked. "Why are we getting so dressed up?"

Allen gave me a grin. "I told you I would pay you back for the upgraded seats. There's something you don't know about Aunt Vi. She's an opera singer, and we'll see her in *The Phantom of the Opera* at the theater tonight as a special guest in box five."

My mouth dropped open. I had always wanted to see *The Phantom of the Opera*, and now I was not only getting to live out one of my dreams, but I would be with Allen, and we had special seats. Allen and I got dressed and then headed down to the cab.

The cab was off, moving quietly as Aunt Vi asked the driver to get us there in a hurry. She then looked at me. "I hope you like the surprise, darling. Allen worked so hard on it."

Allen smiled. "He knows, Aunt Vi, I told him while we were getting ready."

She frowned. "Oh, I wanted it to be a surprise when I walked on stage."

Allen and I laughed. "It's all right; I'm so excited for the show and to see you perform," I said with a smile as big as a Cheshire cat.

Aunt Vi smiled back and gave Allen a wink. How odd it was that she winked at him; what else did these two have up their sleeves?

When we arrived at the theater, I saw there was a poster on the side of the building. Now playing The Phantom of the Opera, with our leading lady Violet Fraser, and with a special opening act for tonight only by Allen Fraser.

I looked at them both, then asked, "Vi, are you the leading lady, and Allen, you're not the Allen Fraser on the poster, are you?"

They looked at me, and then Aunt Vi said, "Surprise, darling, we meant for you to find out that we were coming to the opera, but I pulled some strings, and Allen is going to open tonight. He is a wonder violinist, and he told me you didn't know that."

I was in shock. I thought I knew Allen, and now I was finding out he was a violinist; how did none of our friends know this? We headed inside. Allen and Vi took me to my box before rushing off to get ready. I had the box to myself, and I was happy with that. I didn't even think about texting Anthony any of this as I knew he would get upset; I was waiting for the curtain to rise and to see Allen.

The curtain started to rise, and the theater filled with applause. In a second, Allen was standing on stage, and the orchestra was at the ready in the pit below. The conductor raised his arms, and the orchestra started. A moment later, Allen changed his stance, looked at box five, and started playing. I was in amazement when I recognized the song, "Stand by Me." For the whole song, I kept my eyes locked on him, and he played with such passion and grace, never once looking away from the box. My heart was racing. These past few days had been perfect. We had held hands, he'd confided in me his feelings about not being true to himself, and now I was sure he was serenading me. I was falling in love with him, and something was telling me he was falling for me as well. When the song finished, the room filled with an explosion of claps and cheers. I stood up from my chair and clapped and clapped as I watched him take his bow. Once the applause stopped, he gave an encore. He put his violin away and pulled out a cello. I was even more surprised; not only did he play the violin but the cello also. He was indeed a talented musician. In a flash, Vivaldi Winter was ringing in the walls of the theater. I watched as he played one of the most influential pieces of music. He and the orchestra made it seem so easy.

When he had finished his performance, Allen stood from his chair, took a bow, and ran off the stage. I was waiting for him to enter the box; I wanted to hug him badly. I really wanted to kiss him, but I was with Anthony, and I still didn't know if he felt the same for me as I did him. Once I saw him, I grabbed him and hugged him, and he held me tightly back. "That was amazing. I was so moved. I cannot believe you've never told anyone about your ability to play."

He smiled. "I didn't think our friends would understand, and Anthony was already unstable." He stopped. "I'm sorry. I shouldn't have said that about him."

I smiled and brushed it off. We sat to watch as Aunt Vi took the stage. She looked up at us, blew a kiss, and the show began.

Aunt Vi and the actor playing the Phantom were excellent. The energy they shared on stage made the whole performance and story come to life right in front of us. I had been to plays and operas in the past where the leads didn't seem to like one another, but not this time. I really saw myself in Paris as the story unfolded. My favorite part was when Aunt Vi and Raoul were standing on top of the opera house and singing "All I Ask of You." During this time, Allen's hand was once again reaching for mine, and without a word, I took it and held it as Aunt Vi and her counterpart sang and professed their love for one another. We held hands for the rest of the show, only letting go to applaud when necessary. When the final curtain fell, we both rose from our seats and clapped and cheered for Aunt Vi and her performance; again, she blew a kiss, and we blew them back.

After the cast had left the stage, Aunt Vi came to the box with the actors who played the Phantom and Raoul. We had a pleasant conversation about how they got into acting. They praised Allen for his performance before we said our goodbyes. Aunt Vi went out to dinner with the cast and sent Allen and me to Ognisko around the corner from the theater as a treat from her. Dinner was delightful; many patrons from the show were also dining there, and some even came up to congratulate Allen on his performance and ask if he would ever be playing again. Allen was always polite. He would tell them it had been for one night only, he was afraid. This saddened many, and they asked him to reconsider, but when we told them that he was from America and here on vacation, they would usually understand and leave us be. I could not take my eyes off him; I wanted to tell him how I felt and confess my love for him right there, but what about Anthony and our relationship? I wanted to make it work, but lately, he seemed distant and more irritated when we talked.

After dinner, we hailed a cab and returned to Aunt Vi's home for our final night. When we arrived, she was not home yet. We went to the bedroom, and I felt confident and stripped down right in front of Allen; he just stared. I stared back and he, too, stripped down. We were both standing in our underwear when we heard the door close and Aunt Vi's voice. "Boys, are you home?" she called up the stairs.

Allen responded, "Yes, we just got back and are changing."

We heard her voice again. "Well, don't be long. I'll put on a pot of tea and be out of my room shortly. I would like to spend some time together before you two leave tomorrow morning."

Allen and I smiled, put on some clothes, and headed to the parlor.

The night was wonderful; we had tea and drinks, played parlor games, and talked about the trip and the show. At one point, Aunt Vi was looking down.

"What's wrong, Aunt Vi?" Allen asked.

"Oh, it's nothing, darling; I've had so much fun these last few days and just wish you two could stay longer."

Allen hugged her, and I felt bad we had to leave her. I wished we could stay longer, too, but I also wanted to see my family. "It's okay, Vi, we'll return with my family to Scotland. I'll be back, and Allen will always be welcome to come with."

Aunt Vi smiled. "Oh, you're so sweet, David. Allen, I wish you could find someone as great as David. Is there no one, dear?"

You could feel the tension in the room. Allen was looking back and forth between us. He finally said, "I'm afraid I haven't had much success in the romance world, Aunt Vi; the women in America are so much different from here."

She sighed. "Oh, that's a shame, dear."

After that, we returned to our parlor games to improve the mood of the evening. We played late into the night before Aunt Vi looked at her watch. "Oh my, look at the time; we must be getting to bed if we want to get up in time to get you two to the airport."

We all got up, said our goodnights to Aunt Vi, and headed to bed. Once back in the room, Allen stripped back down to his underwear and hopped into bed. I stripped down and headed to the shower.

I heard the door open. "David, are you okay?" Allen said in a concerned voice.

The truth was I was feeling down; I was sad to leave tomorrow. I was sad about Anthony and worried about how fast my feelings were growing for Allen, knowing I would end up hurt. "Yeah, I just wanted a hot shower before our travels tomorrow."

With that, I heard the door close, and he walked back down the hall. I finished my shower and walked back to the room. Allen was asleep, so I made sure to be quiet so as not to wake him. As I climbed into bed, I grazed his chest with my hand; his muscles were firm and pleasing. I felt my heart beating fast as I got settled. I reached over for my phone and texted Anthony.

I missed you today. I hope you're okay. I can't wait to return to your arms in a few days.

I wanted to see if he would respond, but nothing. I closed my eyes, rolled over, put my arm around Allen, and went to sleep.

Chapter 14
VACATION IN SCOTLAND

We had only a few hours of sleep before the alarm went off to wake us up for our trip. I was up right away, but Allen was struggling to get up. I started packing our bags while he slept, and once we were all packed, I shook him. "Allen, it's time to get up; we have a plane to catch." He moaned and rolled over. I don't know what came over me, but I smacked his ass as hard as possible and yelled, "Wake up!"

With that, Allen was up and looking at me. "What was that for?" he asked in a dazed manner.

"I'm sorry, but I let you sleep past the alarm; I even tried to shake you, so when you showed me your ass, I took the chance in front of me."

He smiled, then laughed, and with that, he was out of bed and soon dressed. We headed downstairs to find Aunt Vi had made a massive spread for us. There were eggs, sausages, bacon, scones, crumpets, and an assortment of sweets.

"Oh wow, Aunt Vi, this is amazing," Allen said with wide eyes.

"Oh, I know, darling. I couldn't sleep last night and wanted you boys to have a proper breakfast before you leave today," she said in a sad voice.

We all ate, and once done and the kitchen cleaned, we headed off. Aunt Vi rode to the airport to see us off, and we hugged and said our goodbyes at the gate. Aunt Vi had tears in her eyes as we walked into the terminal.

Our flight to Scotland was short, and when we arrived in Glasgow, Mum and Dad were waiting for us in the baggage claim area.

"David, we are so happy to see you," Mum said as she ran up to me and hugged me.

Dad strolled over, hugged me, then looked at Allen and shook his hand. "We have quite a drive to get home, guys. Let's get your bags and get going," Dad said in his typical monotone voice.

We gathered our luggage and headed to the car for the long drive back to the village. I looked out the window as we drove. Seeing familiar sights, I knew we were getting closer to home, and I was feeling excited to see Sam and introduce her to Allen. Still, I was also nervous to see my grandparents and see how Allen would react to my small village. I decided to text Anthony.

Landed in Scotland. Mum and Dad picked us up from the airport; it was great to see them. I'm looking forward to seeing my grandparents and friends again. I wish I could have brought you to my village.

Anthony replied with one of his now all too often short responses.

Glad you made it. Have fun.

Again, his answers made me feel bad that I'd come here with Allen and that he was still mad about it. I touched down when Allen reached over and put his hand on my shoulder; at this point, we had come up to the road leading to my village.

We pulled into the drive of our family home, and my grandparents were sitting out front waiting for us. I exited the car, walked up to them, and hugged them both.

"It's so good to see you, darling; we've missed you around here," said Grandma in her sweet voice.

Granddad was quiet, and I could tell he was observing Allen. "This is my mate from school, Grandad. I made a bet with him that he wouldn't last one day on the farm. We'll be out early tomorrow morning to work."

At this, Grandad's eyes lit up; the thought of me coming to work on the farm and bringing free labor made him smile. He hugged me and said he was glad I was home. We all went into the house. Mum made tea for everyone, and we all chatted together about our trip, about the sights we saw and the things we did. When it came to our last night, we didn't tell them about Allen's performance; we just told them we went to see a musical.

"Well, it sounds like you two have been having so much fun. Hopefully, Allen, you will find just as much enjoyment in our village of Morven as you did in London," Grandma said.

Grandad said, "Ah, all we need here in our village is clean air and a good work ethic; what more fun could anyone need?" He smiled and sat back in his chair like he had just won a great debate.

"Oh, don't listen to them," Mum said. "We have plenty of sights and things to do. I'm sure David can show you all the fun spots." She smiled sweetly at Allen.

Dinner was ready, so we all headed into the dining room. Being home with my family and having dinner around the table was excellent. Afterward, we saw Granddad and Grandma off, and Allen and I went to my room to get ready for bed as we had to be up early for a day of work on the farm.

Morning came, and when I say it was morning, the sun wasn't even up yet. I climbed out of bed and put on my farm clothes. I also pulled some out for Allen, as I was sure he had nothing suitable. Once Allen was dressed, we headed out to Grandad's farm. When we arrived, the sun was coming up over the horizon, and Grandad and his crew were at the barn waiting for us.

"Good morning, boys. Today we're herding the sheep out to the far pasture. Allen, you know how to ride a horse?" he asked with a grin, knowing this would be a fun day.

To our surprise, Allen said, "I ride horses all the time back home. I should be fine."

Again, Allen had impressed me. I thought I knew everything after our time in London, but he still found ways to amaze me. We mounted our horses and waited for the gate to open to start our trip to the upper pasture. The ride wasn't short; I used to take it all the time with Grandad and was used to it, but for Allen, the five-mile trek up the hillside seemed to be getting to him.

I rode up next to him. "Are you okay, Allen?" I asked quietly so the others wouldn't hear.

"I'm fine. I just wasn't expecting such a long ride right after our trip."

I smiled. "I told you farm life wasn't easy when we made the bet."

Allen gave me a look and a side grin as though to say, *you're in for it when I get a chance*. We made it to the pasture, and once the sheep were in and the gate was closed, Grandad released Allen and me back to the farm, saying he and the guys would finish up.

I looked at Allen and said, "Want to race these horses back?"

Allen looked at me and smiled, and without a word, he and his horse bolted off. I grinned and sent my horse into a full-speed gallop back, not for a moment letting up. We raced, laughing the whole way. Once we reached the barn, we unsaddled the horses and went up to the house to check on Grandma.

Grandma would be in the kitchen, this was no surprise to me as this is where one could usually find her. "Oh, hello, David and his friend. I'm sorry, dear, I forgot your name. I just finished a pie. Should be cool enough to eat in a minute."

Walking over I kissed her on the cheek. "His name is Allen, Grandma, and some homemade pie sounds lovely."

She gave one of her sweet smiles, "Of course, Allen, I'm sorry. How was your first time on a farm, dear?"

Allen glanced over at me with a side smile before turning his attention back to my grandma. "I had a great time. Seeing how sheep herding works was nice."

She smiled as she moved around the kitchen getting things ready for the pie. "Well, we hope to leave the farm to David once he's done with school, and hopefully the young lady he marries will also be able to help. We have hope for his friend Sam; have you met her?"

I felt sick inside. "No, Grandma, we haven't had a chance to see Sam yet. Hopefully later today. I need to call her."

She glanced over at me, then at Allen who was bringing the pie to the table. "Well, why don't you go give her a call? Allen can help me get the pie cut and served."

I agreed and walked into the other room to call her. I pulled out my phone and dialed Sam. It rang once before I heard her voice. "David, hi, how are you?"

"I'm well. I'm back in Scotland at my grandparents' farm."

I could hear her excitement. "Oh my god, David, I can't wait to see you. We should have dinner tonight. I can't wait to hear all about your time in America."

I smiled. "Yeah, that sounds fun. I brought a mate; he can't wait to meet you."

Her voice changed to a more *David, you naughty boy* tone. "You brought your boyfriend home with you?" she asked.

"Oh no, he's not my boyfriend; he went to see his family on holiday. Allen is just my good mate."

We chatted for a bit more, decided on a time for dinner, and hung up.

When I entered the kitchen, Grandma and Allen had the pie cut and plated on the table, and the tea kettle had just finished boiling. I sat down and filled Allen in on our plans to have dinner with Sam, who was excited to meet him. Grandma smiled at this. The three of us ate the pie and talked about how things had been since I left and how Grandad was doing. Grandma talked about her charity work in the village and some local gossip. It was an enjoyable visit; I missed my grandma and was happy to be there with her. After everything was all cleaned and put away, Allen and I returned to the house to get ready for our dinner with Sam.

Once in my room, the clothes came flying off the both of us. I forgot what the smell of horse and sheep was like and wanted out of those clothes, and I think Allen did as well. I let him shower first, and once he was out and back in my room in just a towel, I went and showered before he had the chance to drop his towel and I saw him naked again, like back in London. After the shower, I returned to find that Allen had not gotten dressed; he was just in his underwear. I enjoyed the sight but didn't want it to become obvious, so I looked at him in the eyes and said, "Is everything okay? You haven't gotten dressed yet."

He looked at me. "Oh, well, I didn't know how dressed up I needed to get," he said with a sly smile.

There was no way he didn't know the village was not large and not fancy in any manner. We didn't have many restaurants or places to hang out, and everything we did have was just your regular place. He purposely wanted me to see him this way, but I just said, "Oh, jeans and a jumper are fine. We're just going to the local pub, which is a real one, unlike that one in America you took me to after football practice."

Allen smiled and laughed before getting dressed.

The pub was a short walk down the street, and we were there in about five minutes. When we arrived, Sam was already there waiting outside for us. "Oh my god, David," she yelled as she ran up and hugged me. "I am so glad to see you. I've missed you so much."

I smiled and hugged her tightly. "I missed you so much, too. We have so much to catch up on." I let go of her and turned to Allen. "This is my mate Allen from America," I said, bringing him closer to introduce him to Sam. They both smiled, said hello, and we headed into the pub. Walking in was like old times after a long day on the farm when we would come here to relax; the smells and the sounds brought back many good memories. The three of us headed to a booth and ordered a round of drinks and some food.

Sam and I were chatting and catching up while Allen sat there. She looked over at him. "So you haven't said much. Tell me, Allen, how did you and David meet, and how have you become such good friends?"

Allen had a look of panic on his face; I thought it was funny that he was feeling uncomfortable about Sam and her questions. I chimed in to save him. "We live in the same building and play on a football team together, and we have some mutual friends who are dating and also live in the same building, so it just kinda happened, I guess."

The panic on his face started to fade, and Sam smiled. "And what of this boyfriend, David? Why did he not come along? I was looking forward to meeting him."

I froze. I'd hoped we would be able to talk about that more in private, but Allen finally spoke. "Oh, Anthony is with his family, and I asked David to come with me on the trip to London. Coming home was a last-minute thing, so he didn't have time to ask Anthony to change his plans."

Sam smiled at Allen, and we went back to general conversation. We drank and laughed the rest of the night and had a good time; it was great to see Sam again. Allen was putting on the charm with her, and she was eating him up. I was pretty jealous of how well they were getting along and afraid they might like each other.

We went to leave a few hours later. We waited for Sam's ride to get her, and then as Allen and I had a little to drink, we stumbled and laughed as we walked back home. Once back at the house, we tried to enter quietly so as not to wake my parents. Dad was sitting in the parlor. "Oh boys, good, you're home safe. Well, I'm off to bed. Goodnight." With that, he walked to my parents' room.

Allen and I stumbled up the stairs to my room, where we got undressed and fell into bed. We lay there talking about the day, about how I was amazed at how well he did on the farm, and how I was glad he and Sam got along. We talked about our plans for the following day and the sights I wanted to show him. I don't know what came over us, but Allen leaned in. We were sitting with our foreheads together with our arms around one another, and then he kissed me. This sobered us both up fast, and he quickly realized what he had done and jumped out of bed. "Oh my god, David, I am so sorry," he said in a panic. "We're drunk, and I don't know what that was all about."

I smiled and laughed. "It's okay, Allen, get back in bed and go to sleep. We can forget about it."

He sighed, got back into bed, and went to sleep. I lay there; my mind was racing. Allen kissed me, something I had wanted, but what about Anthony? What would he think about this when I told him? I had to tell him about it; it was our deal to be truthful, but how would he handle it? Would he be mad? I was getting anxious about this and tried to sleep but instead tossed and turned all night.

I woke before Allen the following morning and headed downstairs to the kitchen. Mum was making breakfast when I entered.

"Good morning, David, the kettle just finished. Make yourself a cup of tea, and I'll have food ready soon. Has your friend woken up yet?"

I made myself some tea. "Not yet. Allen tends to sleep in late if you let him."

Mum chuckled. "Well, Grandad rang last night to tell me what help you two were with the sheep. I'm sure it was his way of saying, 'See, David can run the farm,' but it was nice of him to ring."

I smiled. I did have fun yesterday on the farm, but that was because Allen was there, but I didn't want to tell Mum that. She finished cooking, and we sat down at the table together.

"So, your father had to leave for his office, and Allen is still sleeping; we can now talk, just the two of us," Mum said with a smile. "How are things, darling? Are you happy in America?"

I looked down at my food. "I'm enjoying the experience and I love studying, and I have my friends Allen, Alessia, and Mark," I said, still not wanting to look up. "I've started talking to someone, and we were getting more serious, but I don't know. Things have been weird between us lately." I glanced up to see Mum was fully invested, giving me a look of love and concern.

"Now, David, you know you can tell me anything; what makes you think this way?"

I frowned. "Well, he wasn't too happy that I came on this trip with Allen." I froze after this. I just said *he*. I hadn't told my parents yet, and now I'd just said he when telling my mum what was bothering me. I waited in suspense for her to respond.

"Well, he seems to have some issues to work out. Allen seems like a lovely boy, and I know you're not one to mess things up with someone you care about."

I looked at her. "You're not surprised it's a guy?" I asked quietly.

"Oh, David darling, your father and I have known for years; we were waiting for you to tell us. Grandma knows too; she thought Allen was your boyfriend. The only one who doesn't have a clue is your grandad." She stood up from her chair, walked over to me, and hugged me. "We love you, David, and we just want you to be happy. I knew going to America would help you understand your sexuality, and I'm glad you did and found someone."

I sighed. "There's another thing: I have feelings for Allen, and he's straight, but this trip, we've grown closer, and last night after the pub, he kissed me in a drunken state, and he and Anthony, my boyfriend, don't get along."

Mum looked at me. "Oh, well, that is a problem, dear, and you will have to figure out the best outcome."

When she heard Allen coming down the stairs, Mum went to fix him a plate, and I made myself a fresh cup of tea.

Allen entered, and we all said good morning. Mum sat his plate on the table next to mine, he made a cup of tea, and we all ate. We finished our breakfast together, and after we helped clean up the kitchen, Mum asked what our plans were for our last day here.

"First, I want to take him down to see Kinlochaline Castle, then I thought we could take Grandad's boat to the Isle of Mull, see some of the old castles and sites, and then have lunch there."

Mum smiled. "That sounds like a lovely plan. I'll have Grandad ready the boat. I have to go to the isle myself anyway for business so I can sail with you two and we can go past Ardtornish Castle and the lighthouse and land over at Craignure Bay. I can have two cars waiting, one for you boys to drive around the island and one to take me to my meeting, and we can then meet at the Isle of Mull Rugby Club for lunch with your father and watch the match before sailing home in the evening."

With our plans made, Allen and I went upstairs to dress and head for Kinlochaline Castle. We took the car to make it faster. The castle was a short drive from home, only about five minutes. I could see his amazement at something so old and majestic on his face, and he looked at me and said, "I have lived in major populated cities all my life; I never knew that there were things like this still out here. I thought they were just past ruins in books."

I laughed. "Well, I thought the world was mostly small villages, aside from some major cities, till I came to America, so I guess we both were wrong."

We laughed and jumped out of the car to explore the castle grounds. I always loved coming here as a child and even imagined bringing my love here one day to propose in front of the castle overlooking the river. Now, I was here with Allen, which was just as grand. We spent a good hour or so looking around before we headed back to the car to meet Mum at the boat to head over to the Isle of Mull.

The boat was kept in Lochaline Harbour, and when we arrived, Mum and Grandad were waiting for us. "Ah boys, there you are, she's all ready to go. David, I am trusting you with her as Mum is not the best sailor, you know, and Allen, I know you can handle a horse, but a sailboat is much different," Grandad said with a chuckle.

"We'll be fine, Grandad. Mum is helpful, and I'm sure Allen will get the hang of it once we're out in the open."

With that, we boarded the boat, Grandad tied us loose, and we headed off. The day was perfect for sailing, and a nice breeze gave us a reasonable speed. Soon, the castle and lighthouse of Ardtornish were in sight. Allen was looking again in amazement like he had back at Kinlochaline. Mum saw this and laughed. "Allen, are you amazed that David lives near so many castles?"

Allen smiled at her. "I am just amazed they're still standing after all these years."

Mum sat there for a second before she responded. "Well, the Scottish love our history, and we try very hard to preserve it and our slower pace of life."

Allen gave her a smile and looked over at me again with a glint in his eyes I had not seen before. Soon we were turned and headed down to the bay; the water was rougher than expected, but Mum and Allen followed my directions, and we made it to the bay without any issues in no time.

Once the boat was tied up, Mum showed us to the cars. We said our goodbyes and headed off. I decided to take him over to Duart Castle; this way, we would also drive by Torosay Castle, allowing Allen to see more of the historic castles and beauty of the Northing Highlands. While driving, Allen said, "You amaze me, David; I had no idea you knew how to sail."

I smiled. "Well, there's not much opportunity to sail back in Ann Arbor now, is there?"

Allen gave a small chuckle. "I guess you're right, but the way you handled the boat and the waters, I was just amazed that you did it with two people who have no clue what to do on a boat."

I gave out a laugh at him, "Well, you amazed me with your playing in London; I get to amaze you with castles and sailing."

We started the drive to Duart Castle, and Allen again had his face pressed to the window, taking it all in.

Once the car was parked, Allen jumped out and started looking around. I was watching him when my phone started to ring. I looked at it; Anthony was calling. I had not thought about him at all this morning, or how I would tell him about what happened the night before, so I answered, "Hey, babe, how are you?"

Anthony sounded much happier. "Hey babe, I'm great. I'm just starting my trip back to Ann Arbor. How are you? I can't wait to see you tomorrow when your plane lands." This was nice; he had been so distant this past week, and now he was being attentive and kind again. I guess the family stress was over for him, and he could relax.

"Great. Mum and I had a friendly chat this morning, and I told her about us, then we sailed to one of the isles near home, and Allen and I are exploring castles."

Anthony's demeanor changed at the mention of Allen. "Well, I'm glad you and your mom could talk. That's great." He then said in a more serious tone in his voice than before. "Has Allen caused you any trouble?"

"No, he's been behaving himself," I said.

"Well, that's good. I have to go. We're getting to the airport. I'll text you when my plane takes off."

We said our goodbyes, and we hung up.

Allen came running over. "Who was that? Everything okay?"

I smiled. "It was just Anthony; he was letting me know he was getting to the airport and would text me when his plane takes off."

Allen's expression turned from happy to panicked. "You didn't tell him about last night, did you?"

I gave him a puzzled look of confusion. "Oh, I figured we would just forget that happened. No, I didn't tell him, but I plan to when we get home; it's our deal not to hide things from each other. I'm sure he'll understand."

Allen looked nervous. "Yeah, you're right; let's forget about it and enjoy our day," he said, trying to end the conversation. I smiled, and he headed off to explore the castle.

After we had explored every possible corner, it was time to drive to the rugby club, so we got into the car and headed off. Our drive was quiet for the most part, Allen looking out the window and taking in the picturesque surroundings of the country and me in my thoughts. I had not been feeling as anxious or depressed as I had before the trip, but the idea of seeing Anthony and telling him about what happened was making me so. I felt sad. I felt bad that I allowed it to happen, and I felt terrible thinking about how Anthony might feel. He didn't care for Allen, that much was clear, and to find out that he kissed me when he rejected him when he tried to kiss him…

How would he handle that, how would this affect our already rocky relationship? All these thoughts were running around and around in my head, and I could not settle myself. Hopefully, lunch with Mum and Dad and the rugby match would take my mind off things, even if just for a little while.

Once at the club, we found Mum and Dad sitting there waiting for us out front.

"Hello, boys. Ready to watch what's more like what you Americans call football, Allen?" Dad said in a joking manner. I smiled at this as Dad always tried to ensure everyone he met felt comfortable around him.

Allen smiled back. "I don't know if rugby is like football in America, Mr. Ricci, but I look forward to it." With that, we headed inside to grab lunch before the match started.

Lunch was a nice spread; there were many salads, fish dishes, sandwiches, pies, and a table of sweets. The four of us talked about what Allen and I had been up to today and the sights we saw. Dad talked a little about his business on the isle, as did Mum, but they didn't go into much detail; it turned out Dad had been at the rugby club all day, as this match was a charity event and the client wanted to make sure all the legal paperwork was in order before the event started for any last minute donations to the organization. Once we finished our lunch, we headed off to the field to watch the rugby match.

The match was an intense one; they had some up-and-coming players, some retired players, and some who were currently playing for professional teams, but all of them were fierce, and even the older players made the young ones look like rookies, which made for a great match. Allen was watching and looked to be enjoying himself. I was glad that this part of our trip was just as exciting as London. I could now relax knowing that he had fun. Once the match had finished, Dad took the three of us down to the field to meet some of the players. We congratulated them on a great game before heading back to the bay to sail home. This time, I would have Dad help me so things would go a lot smoother than our sail over, as Mum had decided to drive Dad's car back home instead of coming on the boat with us.

The sail back was uneventful; the winds were in our favor, and the waters calm. We made it past the lighthouse again and up to the harbor to put Grandad's boat back in its slip. Once it was all tied and secured, the three of us jumped in the car to head home, but Dad explained that we were due at my grandparents' for dinner as a family before Allen and I left the next day. We drove to the house to find Mum had beat us there, and the three of them were waiting for us in the parlor. We all said our hellos and chatted for a bit about the day. Grandad was concerned for his boat; once we assured him it was fine, we headed into the dining room for dinner.

Dinner was pleasant. Grandad took his chance to talk about the farm and the work Allen and I did in one of his famous attempts to get me to reconsider university and take over the farm. Grandma talked about her charity work around the village, Mum and Dad talked about the rugby match, and everyone was laughing and getting along, unlike before I left for university when Dad and Grandad could not stop fighting.

My phone buzzed. Anthony's text was, *Sorry, forgot to text you when the plane took off. I'm back home and safe. I'll pick you and Allen up tomorrow when your plane lands. Xoxo.*

I put my phone away when my Grandma asked, "Who was that, dear?"

I looked up, startled. "Oh, it was my friend Anthony. He's picking Allen and me up from the airport in America tomorrow and was just double-checking the time."

Grandma just smiled and returned to her conversation with Mum. Allen looked over at me with an accusatory expression. I gave him a look to say, *we will discuss it once in my room tonight.*

The rest of the dinner was uneventful. Afterward, Grandma brought out pies she made for dessert and a pot of tea, and we headed into the parlor to have it so Grandad could smoke his pipe.

Once back home and in my room, Allen was angry. "Why is he picking us up? I thought you were going to have Alessia do it?"

I looked at him with a sad expression. "I'm sorry; I was going to have her do it, but she and Mark will only be home a few hours before we land, and I didn't want to put that on her. Besides, I want you and Anthony to get along. I care a lot about the both of you, and I don't want you two fighting all the time; it stresses me out, and I can't handle it."

Allen sat on the bed and gestured for me to sit next to him. I did but with caution, and he put his arm around me. "I'm sorry, I'm just stressed that you're going to tell him I kissed you. I know he's not going to handle it well, and I care for you, David. I don't want to see you hurt."

I smiled and leaned my head on his shoulder. "I'm sorry too. I've had so much fun this week with you, and I don't want to ruin our friendship over something as minor as Anthony picking us up from the airport."

Allen looked at me. "David, this would not ruin our friendship. I would never let that happen. I like who I'm becoming because of you. Don't ever feel down because of me."

This made me feel good inside but anxious about tomorrow. With that, we stood up, undressed, and got into bed. I again had another sleepless night thinking about what tomorrow would bring once back in America.

Chapter 15
REUNITED

We had to be up early to drive back to Glasgow to catch our plane back to America. When I upgraded our seats for our flight out, I was able to get business class again, so our check-in process would be much faster and more straightforward, giving us the extra time to say goodbye to my grandparents and Mum before Dad drove us to the airport. On our way there no one talked much, and once there Dad hugged me, shook Allen's hand, and off we went into the airport. Thankfully Glasgow is nowhere near as busy as the DTW in America and we were through check-in pretty fast. Once at our gate, Allen and I sat down and waited for our flight to board. He was on his phone like before, and I had my nose in a book. Boarding started, and we got in the queue at the ticket counter and were soon in our seats. It didn't take long before the plane was in motion, and we were in the same situation as before, Allen's hand in mine as the plane took off then relaxing once we were cruising. This time the skies were calm so I didn't get to hold his hand as much. Before we knew it we were descending and getting ready to land. We went through the procedure of holding hands, touched down, and went to baggage claim.

As we entered baggage claim, I saw Anthony standing there. When he saw me, he came running over, picked me up, spun me around, and kissed me.

Allen walked up. "Hey, Anthony, good to see you."

Anthony just looked at him and grabbed my hand. We walked to the conveyor and waited for our bags. You could cut the tension with a knife; Anthony and Allen would not look or even talk to one another. I tried to get them to chat, but nothing. The bell rang, and bags started to come down. Our bags took longer than usual, and with each passing moment, the tension between them grew. Anthony held my hand tighter each time he saw Allen looking at us. It was pleasant, I admit, to be holding his hand, but the fact it was clear it was to mess with Allen made me feel bad. Our bags arrived, and we collected them and headed for the exit. As we walked out, Anthony asked about our trip, what we did, and how things went with my parents and meeting Allen's aunt. I kept it short so we would have something to talk about with Alessia and Mark at dinner that night. I could also tell it made Allen uncomfortable.

The ride home was just as uncomfortable as waiting at baggage. I was feeling bad for putting Allen through this, and the fact that he and Anthony weren't even trying to talk and get along was making me more upset. I wanted to put it from my mind and think about how nice it would be to see Alessia and hear about her trip with Mark. I was sure it was beautiful. I was also starting to miss Sam and my family. I wanted to go back to the UK. I had been much happier there this past week, and I wanted to stay in that happiness, but now I was faced with having to tell Anthony about the kiss and see how this was going to affect everything. I hoped it went well and he would understand that it just happened and that I didn't ask for it.

Thankfully, we were almost back to my apartment. Anthony parked the car, grabbed my bag, and we all headed inside. We climbed into the elevator and went to my floor. I said bye to Allen and that would see him at dinner tonight. We headed to my apartment, and Anthony and I went inside.

I turned to him and was going to tell him about the kiss, but before I could get a word out, his lips were on mine, and he was kissing me deeply. We made out for a few minutes before finally pulling away. I excused myself to the bathroom. Once inside, my heart was racing, and I was feeling a panic attack coming on. How was I going to tell him when he clearly missed me? I didn't want to hurt him, but I was afraid that if I kept it any longer, it could be a more significant issue when it was really nothing. How could I be so stupid to allow this to happen? I didn't want to hurt Anthony, but I couldn't lie about my feelings for Allen.

Once I calmed myself, I went back out into the living room. Anthony was sitting there on the couch with two cups of tea. I was amazed as he had never made me tea before. What was he up to? And what had he done with the real Anthony?

"Oh David, I made tea. I hope I did it right. Come sit. I want to hear about your mum and how she took the news of us."

My heart sank; how could I tell him it was a slip-up? I'd told her that I was having doubts about us. I smiled and looked at him. "She said she already knew I was gay and was just happy that I'd found someone." He smiled at this, and I knew I was off the hook; I didn't lie to him. Mum did say something like that. "So, how was your family? Did you tell anyone about me?" I asked, knowing the answer already.

He looked at me. "I told my old friend about us, the one I let you know I was going to see, but not my family."

I just smiled. "Well, maybe next time I can come along."

He looked away, and we just chatted about school and upcoming projects we had before it was time for him to head off to get ready for dinner.

I felt down that I didn't tell him about the kiss with Allen, but also that he didn't tell any of his family about me. Why was he still hiding me from people? What was I doing wrong? The way he acted when I first saw him at the airport and once back in my apartment showed me he missed me, so what was the problem, and how could I fix it?

I walked down to Alessia's apartment to see if she was home as maybe she could give me some insight. I knocked and waited. I could hear her as she made a mad dash for the door. She opened it and squealed. "Oh my god, David, I am so glad to see you."

She pulled me in for a big bear hug, and I smiled and held her tightly. "It's so good to see you, Alessia. We have so much to catch up on before dinner tonight."

With that, she let go and let me in. "Oh, David, what's wrong?"

I smiled and laughed. "It's nothing serious. I need your advice, and I didn't want to bring this up at dinner tonight."

Alessia sat on the couch. "Come sit, tell me all about it," she said with a smile. I smiled as I sat on the couch. "So what's up, babe? How can I be of assistance," she said in a joking manner.

"Well, two things and one is pretty big. First, Anthony still didn't tell anyone about me; he kept me a secret from his family like he was still hiding the fact we're together."

She frowned. "Well, that's just Anthony, and I think you have to take that with a grain of salt at this point; you know he's gonna hide your relationship from people."

I knew she was right, but I hated that fact.

"What's your second issue? Maybe I'll be more help."

I was feeling sick now as I was about to tell someone about Allen and I kissing, and I knew she would take it well, but what if she told Mark? "Well, this one complicates things... Allen and I, we kinda...kissed on our trip one night after we were out drinking."

Alessia just stared. She didn't have a look of surprise or anything on her face; she was just blank. I was starting to feel more anxious. "For the record, he kissed me. I did not engage first, and he immediately regretted it and apologized."

Alessia spoke this time. "Well, that does complicate things. Have you told Anthony?"

I replied, "Not yet. I'm unsure how to tell him or how he'll take it."

Alessia leaned her head on me. "Well, babe, I think you're fucked." We laughed hard at this. "But I think you should tell him before he hears it from Allen. I think it will go better if you tell him."

I knew she was right and agreed, so I went back to my place to get ready for dinner. I took a longer than usual shower; I was tired from the travel, I was upset about Anthony, I was confused about Allen and why he'd kissed me in the first place, and why he and Anthony seemed more hostile than usual. All this was running through my mind while I stood under the water. Once I was done, I went into my room, picked out a nice outfit—some jeans and one of the polos Mum bought me—and headed out. Alessia was in the hall waiting for me, and we headed down together to find Anthony and Mark waiting for us. We all chatted while we waited on Allen. A few moments later, he came out of the elevator, looking as handsome as ever. I was staring, and I think Anthony noticed this as a second later, his hand was in mine. Soon we were all walking out the door to the restaurant.

Dinner was terrific. Mark and Alessia told us about their visit to Texas, the sights and things they did, and how she had a wonderful time. She talked about how Mark's family was a blast. Anthony talked a little about his trip and seeing his family; Allen told them about London and Aunt Vi, how she was happy to see him, and how we had a good time seeing the Tower of London and other sights. He told everyone we saw his aunt perform in *The Phantom of the Opera* but failed to mention his performance, and I smiled at this. I talked about Scotland and how it was nice to see my family, show Allen the historic castles and sights at home, and how we went to the isle to do more sightseeing before having lunch with my parents. Anthony was showing signs of displeasure about our sailing trip, but I didn't care; I was having a good time, and Alessia was highly invested and asking all kinds of questions about it, and I didn't want to be rude and not answer her.

With each question and answer, Anthony showed more and more signs of aggravation. Eventually, he stood up and walked off, and we all looked at one another. "Did we say something?" Alessia said.

"I'll go check on him," Mark said as he stood up and chased after Anthony.

Alessia looked at Allen and me sitting across from her. "David, did you tell him about the kiss?"

Allen's eyes widened.

"No, I didn't. I didn't want to make dinner awkward and was planning to after dinner tonight." Allen still looked like a deer in headlights. I looked at him. "I should have told you that I told her, but I didn't see you before dinner. It's okay. She won't say anything."

Allen relaxed a little, and we chatted till Mark came back.

"He's all right; he said he would return in a second. Maybe we change the subject before he gets back." We agreed, and a few moments later, Anthony returned and sat down next to me. I reached out my hand under the table for his, he put his hand in mine, and we continued the night without any more issues, and he and Allen even managed to talk some.

On our way home, we held hands and walked silently. I asked him, "Are you okay? You stormed off at dinner, and I was concerned."

He just glanced at me but didn't respond. We made it back to my apartment. I went into the kitchen to start the kettle for tea and came back into the living area. Anthony was sitting on the couch waiting for me. I sat down and again asked him if we were okay. He grabbed me and started kissing me again; we continued until the kettle was done. I headed into the kitchen and made us tea, and when I returned, Anthony was undressed. I put the tea down, and we did our thing.

Afterward, we got dressed, and I knew I had to tell him. "So there was an incident during my trip that I must tell you about."

Anthony looked at me intently. "What happened? Did Allen do something to you?"

I smiled. "No, no. it's nothing like that. Allen did nothing to me, so to speak, but...he did kiss me during the trip."

Anthony looked like he was about to explode.

"We went out with my friend Sam, and we were drinking, and when we got back to my house, we were sitting in my room in bed, and he kissed me. It meant nothing, and he apologized as soon as it happened."

He went off. "He kissed you?" he yelled. "I can't believe it. Why would he do that, and why didn't you stop him?"

I frowned. "It happened so fast, and it was for a second. It's not like I planned for it to happen."

Anthony stood up and began walking back and forth. "I'm going to confront him."

I tried to stop him, but he pushed me away and ran out the door. I didn't know what to do. I sat there in a panic. What should I do? I texted Mark and Alessia.

Told Anthony about Allen kissing me and he stormed out of the apartment and said he was going to confront him.

Seconds later, they were at my door. We all headed for the floor above, and when we got there, the two of them were in the hall in a shouting match, yelling and calling each other all kinds of names. I was having a full-on anxiety attack, and Alessia stayed with me. In contrast, Mark got between them to stop it from coming to blows. "Allen, go back into your apartment NOW, and I'll deal with you later. Anthony, you come with us; we're going back to David's to settle this."

Anthony was not moving. Mark was getting madder by the second and he finally picked Anthony up, threw him over his shoulder, and carried him back to my apartment.

Once back in my apartment, Mark put Anthony down. "Now you two are going to work this out, and you are not going to go back to Allen's to confront him and make matters worse. Do you understand me?" Mark said in a severe, firm tone.

"Fine," Anthony said sharply.

Mark then looked at me. "Well, work it out."

I looked at Anthony. "I told you already it was a mistake, and it meant nothing. I told you because I didn't want to hide it from you."

Anthony was still outraged. "But you wanted it to happen; I know you like him. You told me before we started dating, and then you took this trip with him after I said I didn't want you to."

I was now getting mad and raised my voice. "You didn't want me to come with you, and you couldn't even tell anyone about me. Allen wanted to cheer me up from you being an asshole."

Alessia held my hand, and Mark stood by Anthony to ensure he didn't do anything stupid. "Oh, so I'm an asshole for not taking you on vacation with me?"

I looked at him, furious. "No, you're an asshole because you keep lying about me; you keep calling me just your friend and not your boyfriend."

Alessia chimed in. "That is pretty shitty, Anthony."

Mark gave her a look. Anthony decided to double down on his anger. "Why would I tell anyone about you? You're not that special, and I don't need to tell the world about you."

I started to get dizzy. Alessia pulled me into my room before I completely broke down crying. I could hear Mark and Anthony talking in the living room. I looked over to Alessia. "I want him out. Tell Mark to get rid of him." She stood up, walked out, and told Mark. I heard the door slam, and a second later, she was back in my room to comfort me. I was curled up in a ball on my bed.

She sat down next to me. "Mark followed him out to make sure he didn't go back to Allen's. I'll make us some tea and be back in a moment." I watched as she got up and walked out of the room. I felt dirty and cheap, and most of all, hurt and heartbroken. My depression was taking over, and I saw darkness again. I did not move until she returned and set the tea on the table next to the bed. She hugged me and walked out. I could hear her doing things around the apartment, waiting for Mark to come back in.

It felt like forever before I heard Mark come back. I could hear him and Alessia talking but not what they were saying. He then entered the room. "Hey buddy, are you okay?"

I just lay there. I didn't want to answer, so I just gave him a half smile.

"Well, Alessia will head back to her place, and I'll go have a talk with Allen. We'll be down the hall if you need us, okay?" With that, he shut the door, and I heard them leave. I just lay there feeling awful and sick. I didn't know what to do, and I felt like I had to throw up but couldn't. I cried myself to sleep.

Chapter 16
CHEATER

For the next few weeks, I was going through the motions, feeling sad and unmotivated. I would go to classes and then head back to my apartment. I was ignoring Allen's calls and texts, and I tried to reach out to Anthony, but he was ignoring me. My grades were suffering, and I was seeing a counselor, but things were not getting better. I was just in a limbo state, not getting better or worse. Mark would check on me in our maths class, but I would assure him I was okay.

Today was different. When I got home, Anthony was standing in front of my door. I walked up to him. "Hey, I've been trying to contact you."

He just looked at me with a blank expression. "Can we go inside?"

I opened the door and let us in. I offered him some tea, but he refused. "I just have to know, do you love Allen?"

I gave him a look of confusion while deep down my stomach was starting to do backflips. "Anthony, I care for Allen, but I'm not in love with him; you're the one I care about."

Anthony sighed. "I'm sorry; I shouldn't have accused you of anything. I know you wouldn't hurt me on purpose. Can we try again?"

"I would like that, but you have to promise me that you'll stop hiding me from the world and not keep anything from me like I didn't hide the kiss from you."

Anthony frowned. "Well, I need to tell you something then. I didn't tell anyone about you back home, as my old friend is an ex, which I did tell you about, remember."

I did not say anything, I just sat there waiting for him to continue. "Yeah, I remember you telling me about your ex and that you would see him."

Anthony looked nervous. "Well, we went on a date while I was home."

Rage began building in me. "You went on a date? What do you mean you went on a date?"

Anthony answered, "Well, I was so upset about yours and Allen's trip that I agreed to go on a date with him. Trevor had no idea about you or why I agreed. I'm so sorry."

I just stared; I had no idea how to respond. Before I knew it, I blurted out, "Get out." Anthony looked at me, and I again said, "Get out." He went to say something, but I said, "I'm sorry, Anthony, I need time to process this, but you just admitted to me that you went on a date with someone on purpose."

He understood and walked out.

I was so hurt and feeling sick again. Alessia and Mark were out, and I needed to talk to someone, so I decided to walk to Allen's apartment. I knocked on his door and waited, but there was no answer. I knocked again. This time, I could hear movement. A few seconds later, Allen answered the door. I lost it; I grabbed him, hugged him tightly, and started to cry. He hugged me back, and we just stood there in the moment, holding each other. I felt comfort in this, and I didn't want it to end.

A few more moments went by, and then Allen said, "Come in; I've been so worried about you."

Once inside, I started to break down again. "I just saw Anthony. We talked and agreed to try again, but then he told me he went on a date with his ex while back home, and that's why he didn't tell anyone about me."

Allen looked furious, like he wanted to go find Anthony and kick his ass, but I knew he wouldn't leave me or do anything that would upset me more. "Oh, David, I am so sorry. I caused all this. I wish I could change that night but I can't, and I am truly sorry. I'm sure Anthony didn't go on a date with him and he was saying that to get back at you for our trip and the kiss."

I looked at him. "Even if that's true, it's a shitty thing to do."

He hugged me again. "I know, but you have to remember he's hurt and people do shitty things when hurt."

I cried into his shoulder. "He asked me if I loved you."

Allen released his grip on me. "He asked that?" he said with a note of panic.

"Yeah, I told him I cared for you but wasn't in love with you."

Allen frowned. "I'm sure it was him needing reassurance that the kiss was my fault and not yours. I wouldn't think much of it. I have a concert later today, do you want to come to help keep your mind off things? You can call Anthony tomorrow, and you two can work it out."

I gave him a half smile. "I'd like that. I'll get ready and meet you in the lobby."

Allen's face lit up at my agreeing to come. "Sounds good. We need to leave in an hour."

I headed off to my place to get ready. I texted Anthony to say I was sorry for how I reacted, and that tomorrow we could talk some more. I then threw my phone on the bed to shower and get ready, and when I returned, there was a text from Anthony.

Hey Trevor, I told David about our date. We've decided to try and make things work. I'm sorry, but I owe it to him to try. When I'm back in town for winter break, I'd like to see you again, but we can't hook up this time. I'm sorry.

I had so many mixed feelings about this. I was mad that he cheated on me, and I was angry that he told me Trevor didn't know about me when it was clear he did. Still, I was also pleased that he told him he wanted to try to make us work. I don't know what made me do it, but I called him.

"Hey David, what's up?" he said in a nonchalant tone.

"Oh, I wanted to call you about the text you sent me."

I could hear the confusion in his voice when he said, "What text? I didn't text you."

I was getting mad. "Why don't you look at your text real quick, the one you meant to send to Trevor."

It went quiet for a moment, and I could sense his shock once he realized the error he had made. "David, babe, let me explain," he started to say, but I cut him off.

"Explain what? How you made me feel like shit because Allen kissed me, or the fact that you're an asshole who thought it was okay to cheat on me, then hid the fact but got mad at me for being truthful, or the fact that you told me Trevor didn't know about me, but it's clear he did. So tell me, Anthony, what do you want to explain?" I was now furious, and my rage was increasing; I didn't want to hear his excuses, and I wanted off the phone. Even though I called him, I now wanted it to be over.

Anthony said, "David, just let me come over and explain, and we can talk this out, okay?"

I frowned. How could he think that was a good idea? "No, Anthony, I don't want you to come over; in fact, I don't want to see you again for the rest of the semester and maybe even after. I need time to process this." I hung up and started to get dressed for the concert. Anthony tried to call a few times, but I didn't answer, and he sent a bunch of texts that I didn't open.

Chapter 17
CONCERT

I met Allen in the lobby and we headed to the concert hall. We had a small chat while we walked there, but I didn't bring up Anthony or his text to Trevor. I didn't want to put him in a rage before his performance. When we arrived, he showed me to my seat. Alessia and Mark were there. This pleased me, as spending time with my friends would surely be able to cheer me up out of this mood that Anthony had put me in. We chatted and laughed for a bit before the show started. It was one of those shows where different music students showed off the pieces they had been studying for the semester, and between each, the professor would talk about the student and their achievements. I was surprised that Allen invited Alessia and Mark as back in London he admitted no one knew about his talents. I leaned over to Alessia to ask about this. "Did Allen invite you?"

She leaned back. "Yeah, it was odd. He was like, do you guys wanna go to a concert tonight? It's weird that he's not sitting with us, right?"

That was it; he would surprise them like he did me in London. I smiled at this. "I guess he must have to help out or something," I said back to her.

At this point, the professor started to speak. "Our last performance is one I'm excited for. He is an excellent musician and even just did a one-night-only concert in London." Alessia looked over at me, but I just smiled and looked back at the stage. "Please welcome to the stage Allen Fraser."

We clapped then Alessia said, "You knew this, didn't you?"

I just smiled. "Sure did, but I only learned he could play in London."

Allen came on stage. "Thank you. I have two songs tonight that I'm honored to play for you; the first is from my trip to London, and the second is how one of my closest friends has been feeling lately." The crowd applauded, and he began.

He started with "Stand by Me" and played it as beautifully as in London. Once we cheered, Alessia leaned over. "This is amazing, and not what I thought Allen was studying."

I leaned back. "I know, but he's so good."

Allen bowed and then started his second song, "I'll Never Love Again." I knew this song was about me and the things going on with Anthony; he played it with such grace and beauty that it made me cry. Alessia put her arm around me to comfort me, and it helped, but I was still sad; I didn't know if I would ever love again, and I didn't know if I wanted to. Allen's song made me feel like I was not worthy of love, and I was mad that he'd brought me here, knowing what I just confided in him about Anthony, knowing this song would hurt me. Weren't there warnings from Anthony that Allen could be heartless and evil? Was he laughing at me as he did with Anthony when he led him on? I wasn't sure, but I felt that it might have been a possibility, and I wanted to know, but I was also afraid that I might be right, that all of this that Allen had done over the past month was him having a laugh at the gay guy as he'd done with Anthony the year prior.

After the performance ended, Allen met the three of us out in the concert hall lobby. Mark and Alessia congratulated him and talked about their surprise to see him there. I hugged and congratulated him, and then the four of us decided we should all go to dinner to celebrate Allen's performance and the end of the semester. We decided on a place close to our apartments, as it was getting late, and we didn't want to walk long distances in the winter air if we didn't have to.

We had just sat at the table when Mark asked, "Has anyone heard from Anthony? I haven't seen him since the fight."

Allen looked like he was going to explode. I quickly spoke up. "Yeah, I spoke to him today. He's fine; we probably won't see him till next term, it looks like."

Allen looked less angry but was clearly still upset. I wondered if he was mad that I didn't tell them the truth as to why we wouldn't be seeing him. Either way, Mark seemed to accept this, which ended the discussion. During dinner, everyone talked about their plans for the break; Alessia was going home and wanted me to spend a few days with her after Christmas. Mark and his family were traveling, so we wouldn't hear from him. Allen's aunt Vi was coming to the States for the holiday, and then they were going off to Japan and Italy for her performances. I thought that was why Alessia wanted me to see her; Allen would also be in Italy, and they didn't know I would find out. We continued our dinner, and afterward, we all walked back to our apartments. Allen came with me to my apartment while Alessia and Mark went to hers.

Once we were settled, I made some tea and sat on the couch next to Allen. "I have to ask you something, and I want you to be completely honest with me."

Allen looked at me, confused. "Yeah, of course," he said while watching me cautiously.

"Tonight, your song choices...the first you played for me in London, and the second I felt was like a jab at me for my and Anthony's relationship issues."

Allen frowned. "David, I played them because they're the pieces I've been practicing; I didn't mean for them to offend you."

I just looked at him. "I'm starting to feel that you're playing with me like you did when you led Anthony on last year."

Allen's face went pale. "How could you say that? I care for you, David. Yes, I messed up with Anthony and must live with that. How could you think I was doing that to you?"

I felt down and gave him a frown. "I'm sorry, it's just, between our trip and the kiss and your music, I let my emotions believe there was more going on than there was."

Allen gave me a look with sadness in his eyes. "You're a good guy, David, and one day you'll find someone who will do anything to make you happy; I promise you that."

We finished our tea, and Allen left for his place to change and prepare for our break.

While packing, I felt down about how things were ending this semester. Anthony and I were not talking, and I'd just made Allen feel bad; maybe I wasn't meant to have relationships, perhaps I was destined to be alone. I was going to miss my friends once back home, but I also thought maybe it would be for the best to have time away, to not think about them and focus on me. Sam would keep me busy; she always found things for us to do. I was not packed and ready to head home till the following term and would be leaving first thing in the morning. I got into bed and went straight to sleep for the first time in forever.

Chapter 18
YOU LOVE ME?

I woke up early, put the bags that I was taking home by the door, and called a cab. A few moments later, there was a knock on my door. I thought it was Alessia or Allen coming to say goodbye before they left. I opened it, but there was no Alessia or Allen; it was Anthony. "Hi," I said in a monotone voice.

"Hi," he said back. "Can I come in?"

I let him into the apartment and asked, "What do you want?"

He looked at me sadly. "I want to talk. I'm not ready to give up on us or our relationship because of some stupid mistake."

I looked at him intensely. "Well, it was a pretty big fucking mistake; I suffered wondering how I would tell you that Allen kissed me, and you were out there in another guy's bed."

Anthony frowned. "I know I messed up bad, David, just please let me try and make it up to you. What will it take?"

I thought about it for a minute. What would it take for me to give him another chance? "You really want to try and make this right?" I asked.

"Yes, just tell me what I need to do, and I'll do it."

I could see that he was serious. "Okay, I have two requests. First, you need to tell people we're together."

He cut me off before I could finish. "Done. I told my mother this morning I was staying here with you."

I didn't react; I just continued with my requirements. "Second, you're to come home with me to Scotland today."

Anthony looked at me like I was crazy. A few moments went by, and I expected him to explain why that wouldn't work, and then he started to speak. "Fine, if that's what it takes, I already have bags packed. I'll be back soon with them." With this, he headed out the door.

After he was gone, I started thinking. Was I really going to take him home to Scotland with me? Was this a good idea? Either way, it was done now, and Anthony was coming. Maybe this would be a good thing; perhaps the magic I felt with Allen when we were there I'd experience with Anthony, perhaps this would bring us closer together, and we would get our relationship back on track. I was starting to feel good about this now.

About twenty minutes had passed, and a notification on my phone let me know the cab had arrived. I started to collect my bags and head down. Once there, I let the driver know I had a few more bags and that we were waiting on another person who should be here any moment. I returned to my apartment, collected my last few bags, turned off the lights, and headed down. When I got back down, Anthony was there and loading his bags. I smiled at him, and we loaded the rest of mine. We entered the cab to head to the airport. It was a quiet drive with some tension between us. Still, I didn't think much of it. At the airport, we loaded our bags, checked in, and then went to security with little difficulty. Things were different at the gate; we talked to one another, unlike with Allen, where we did our own thing. The flight was the opposite, however; there was no talking, hand-holding, friendly gestures, or ordering food for one another. But still, we were enjoying each other's company.

Once we arrived at my home in Scotland, I introduced him to Mum and Dad. I told them he was my boyfriend, and neither were surprised that I'd brought him home with me. We had a nice dinner and went off to bed. It was odd at first having Anthony next to me and not Allen. I tried to cuddle up to him, but it wasn't the same.

During the next few days, everything was beautiful. We were getting along better, the tension was gone, and he had told me the night prior that he loved me and would never do anything again to hurt me. This made me feel nice, but I still had doubts. I was trying not to let my fears and anxiety take over, and I wanted to believe him, but I still had this unease about Trevor.

The following day we spent with Sam. She enjoyed Anthony and how happy I seemed and even told him she approved of him. We went out drinking and to dinner with her a few nights in a row, and they hit it off. Things were going great, and I was starting to forget about Trevor. I was beginning to think less about Allen. I even took Anthony to meet Grandma and introduced him as my boyfriend.

Grandma was pleased to meet him as she was with everyone she met and even more happy that I was honest about him being my boyfriend. The issue was when she asked, "What about that nice boy Allen you brought home on your last break?"

Anthony glared at me, but I kept calm. "Oh, Grandma, Allen was just a friend; I told you that."

She scoffed at this. "Oh dear, I may be an old lady, but I could tell that boy had feelings for you." She then looked at Anthony. "Don't take it personally, dear; I think you're lovely as well, I'm just curious, that's all."

Anthony smiled, but I could tell he was uncomfortable and that this would be a fight later. We spent some time with Grandma before we headed home.

As I predicted, as soon as we were in my room, he turned on me. "Why would she ask about Allen in front of me?" he said in an angry tone.

"I don't know. Grandma has never been one for filters, but she knows Allen is just a friend."

He looked at me. "Yes, but she would prefer him over me."

I put my hand on his shoulder. "Babe, it's fine, let it go. She didn't mean any harm, and besides, I'm with you, and I don't care that others don't like it. I like it."

He smiled at this. "I think I'm gonna go take a shower." And with that, he undressed and headed to the bathroom.

His phone buzzed while he was in the shower. I knew I shouldn't look, but I did anyway. It was Trevor.

Please, Anthony, just talk to me. I love you, and I don't want to lose you for some tacky farm boy from another country. Please return my calls or text me back.

Tacky farm boy? I thought to myself. Why would he think that? Was that how Anthony described me to him? I was offended but thought of a better way to handle it. I heard the shower turn off. I stripped naked and waited for Anthony to enter the room. A few moments later, he came into the room in just his towel and saw me. His eyes widened, and he threw off his towel and jumped on top of me. We spent the rest of the night in a severe sex session, so he had no chance to respond to Trevor. That would show him this tacky farm boy could play these games, too.

We had to get up early the following day as it was Anthony's last day here. Sam and I drove him to the airport, and once we had unloaded his bags from the car, he and I hugged one another tightly. "Thank you for letting me prove to you that I want to make this work," he said in my ear. "I love you, David."

I smiled at this, and we kissed. On the drive home, I kept thinking how nice things had been and that he had just told me he loved me. Still, I started to worry. What if Trevor managed to get him to hook up with him again? I wouldn't be able to handle it a second time, and there would never be trust between us again. I forgave him once but would be utterly heartbroken if he did it again.

The next few days, I sulked around the house and was starting to go into a depressive state once again. I was missing Anthony, Alessia, Mark, and Allen, and I could not wait to tell them how much better things were with Anthony and me. I finally came out of my mood and decided I wanted to get out of this house and go out with Sam for the night, so I texted her, hoping she would be up for the idea.

Let's go out tonight. I need to get out of this house.

Sam instantly responded. *About time. I was wondering if we would see each other again before you headed back to school.*

I smiled, and a second text from her came in.

I'll come around soon, and we can go out.

Sounds good. I'll see you in a bit.

I heard the doorbell, and Mum answered. There was distant chatter I couldn't really hear before she yelled up the stairs. "David, you have a visitor." I smiled at Mum saying that but wondered who it could be. Was Sam here already? I grabbed my jumper and headed down. I was soon overcome with shock when I got to the parlor. Mum was still in there, but she wasn't having a conversation with Sam; she was talking to Allen.

We just stared at each other, neither one of us saying a word or taking our gaze from the other. Mum excused herself to the other room. I didn't know what to do or say; he was staring at me, waiting for me to speak.

"Allen? What are you doing here? You should be in Italy with your aunt."

He didn't say anything. He had a look of fear and worry on his face. "I shouldn't have come," he said with a tone of discomfort in his voice.

I looked at him. "Allen, what's wrong? Why are you here?"

He started to speak. "I just, I...I had to come here, David, to see you. I couldn't wait till you returned to school to tell you I love you."

I stood there in shock as he continued, "I flew around the world this week, David, and I could not stop thinking about you. You asked me why I played those songs. It's because I love you, and I will never love anyone as much as I do you. I came here knowing that I feel you love me too."

We both stood there, not saying a word. I could hear Mum in the kitchen trying to pretend she wasn't listening in on our conversation. My mind was racing. What was I to do? Here was Allen spilling his guts and feelings out to me, telling me he loved me, the one thing I had always hoped for, and Anthony had just told me a few days prior he loved me, and we were getting better.

I could hear Mum still in the kitchen, thinking she was being quiet. "Come on, David, you know what to do. Say it back," she said to herself.

I looked at him. "I love you too, Allen. I've wanted to say that to you since our trip."

I could hear Mum murmur, "Yes!"

I smiled, then continued, "But Anthony and I are trying to make it work."

Allen frowned and started to cry.

I could hear Mum mutter, "Oh, David."

Allen then spoke through his tears. "He will never love you the way I do; he will never treat you the way I will. I promise you that he will hurt you again. I will protect you, David. Let me protect you."

I ran and hugged him, and he held me tightly. We stood there for what felt like forever, just like we were back at his apartment when I told him Anthony cheated on me.

Once he calmed down, I spoke calmly. "I'm going to need some time to think about this, but I promise you I will think about it."

Allen smiled and kissed me out of nowhere, just like the first time; however, he did not stop, and I found myself kissing him back.

We stayed this way for what felt like forever before it finally clicked in my mind that we shouldn't be doing this. I pulled away quickly, and the look on Allen's face said it all. He had this look of confusion and guilt all at the same time.

After a second he finally spoke. "I should get going. I need to check into the inn in town and get settled into my room. I'll call you later." Before I could say anything Allen was out the door and it was closing behind him.

At that moment Mum walked into the room. "Oh David, are you all right, dear?"

I didn't know what to say and just sat there in bewilderment. Mum just kept staring at me so I finally said, "Yeah I'm fine. Sam will be here soon so I'm gonna go and finish getting ready. Let her up when she arrives?"

Mum smiled and with that, I headed back up the stairs and into my room, where I threw myself down onto the bed and screamed into my pillow. Why was my life like this, why did Allen and Anthony have to make this so hard? I wasn't able to stew on this long as a few moments later my door was flung open and in walked Sam with her famous smile and cheer that no one could be sad or mad around.

Chapter 19
A FRIEND'S ADVICE

"David, you tosser, what are you doing in bed? We're going out, remember? There's no way you forgot about me in the little time it took for me to get here," she said with a smile and a playful tone in her voice.

I just smiled and hopped out of bed. "Oh, where are my manners? I am soooo sorry, I did not know I was expecting the Princess of Wales," I said in my poshest English accent, the kind aristocrats have. We both busted out laughing. I grabbed my jumper and we headed down the stairs.

We were still laughing when we made it to the parlor. Mum just looked at us both and smiled, and we let her know we were going to get something to eat and cause havoc on the poor townspeople.

Mum, trying to be funny, said, "I'll be sure when the constable rings to say that he's mad and that I've never had a child in my life."

Sam and I both laughed and out the door we went.

Once at the pub, we found a table and ordered all kinds of food and drinks, and had a grand old time. We talked about our plans for the upcoming term, and what we planned to do the coming summer. She was planning a trip, and I still hadn't decided if I was going to come home or stay in the States yet, and now with this Allen and Anthony drama, I wasn't sure I wanted to go back at all. Just then Sam was looking over my shoulder with a confused look on her face. "David? Is that Allen who just walked in?"

I froze, slowly turned my head, and sure as the sun glows in the morning, Allen was sitting at the bar. I quickly turned back to Sam. "Umm, yeah, that seems to be him," I said, not wanting to draw attention to us.

"Well, what is he doing here? I'm gonna go over there and invite him to sit with us."

I grabbed her arm and pulled her back down into her seat. "NO!" I said a bit too loudly as before I knew it Allen was standing next to our table.

Sam had this wicked look on her face. "Well, hello, Allen, what a surprise to be seeing you here in this fine establishment." She busted out laughing.

Allen smiled. "It's good to see you again, Sam. I was just getting something quick to eat before heading back to where I'm staying."

Sam grinned and my stomach was doing backflips. "Oh? And where are you staying? Our David here failed to mention to me that you were in town, and from my understanding he and I are the only people in the village you know, and I sure didn't know you were here." Sam was looking at me sideways like *boy are you in trouble when we get a chance to talk about this.*

I think Allen must have caught on as he quickly chimed in, "Oh, well, I just got into town and thought it was too late to call and didn't want to be rude. David and I had planned to travel back to school together as I was in London visiting my aunt."

Sam looked back and forth between us. I did not for a second think she thought he was telling the truth. "Well, you're here now so why not join us?"

Allen was quick. "Oh no, you two have fun. I ordered my food to go. We can hang out tomorrow, right, David?"

I was startled by his question. "Oh yeah...tomorrow for sure."

With that, we watched as Allen went back to the bar, grabbed his food, and walked out the door.

Within a second Sam was all over me. "Okay, David, tell me the truth. What is Allen doing here, and why didn't you tell me? I know that him just getting into town was a lie."

I shrank into my chair as low as I could. "He showed up to my place just before you did, and he kinda confessed his love for me, I guess you could say?"

Sam looked at me in confusion. "What do you mean you guess he confessed his love for you? Either he did or he didn't. Come on, David, we're not children anymore."

I guessed now was as good a time as any to fill her in on what happened. "Well...the door rang and Mum said I had a visitor. I assumed it was you since you were on your way over, but when I got into the parlor Allen was standing there, and he let it all spill out that he was in love with me, that he wanted me to leave Anthony and let him be my protector, and then we kinda kissed."

Sam was sitting there with her mouth wide open. I wasn't sure how she was going to respond to this, and inside I was starting to feel sick and like I was going to crawl out of my skin if she didn't speak soon. "Soooo, let me get this right. Anthony left to head back to America and now Allen is here, and he confessed he loved you and asked you to leave Anthony and then you kissed him... What the fuck, David?"

I shrank even lower into my chair, and before I could say anything, Sam continued. "You have two hot and I mean *hot* guys pining after you. I'm jealous over here...but seriously, what are you going to do?"

I felt as little as I ever had before. Yes, Anthony and I had finally started to get our relationship on the right track, but then there was Allen, the man of my dreams. I looked at Sam, who was waiting very impatiently for my response. "I don't know, Sam. I don't have a clue."

Sam frowned. "Well, here's my advice and you're getting it whether you like it or not so just sit there and be quiet while I go on my rant."

I nodded, and with that, she was off. "First off, you're in a relationship with Anthony, and sneaking around and kissing Allen, David, you're better than that. Now as for my advice, Anthony and you have a very unstable relationship, and I don't like him. He hasn't introduced you to any of his family or even told them about you, while Allen took you to London for a holiday to meet his aunt, then flew around the world to tell you he was in love with you. I mean, how much more of a cliché rom-com can it get? Next, Anthony has cheated on you, but Allen hasn't. Your grandparents like Allen so it would be easier to come out to them with Allen as your boyfriend than Anthony, and your parents like Allen more than Anthony, but they would never say that as they want you to live your own life." She finally stopped to take a breath, while I just continued to sit there still confused and feeling bad about myself. Sam looked at me. "Oh David, I didn't mean to make you feel bad, I just wanted to be honest. Allen is the much better choice for you, honey, and I just want what's best for you my friend just like you do for me."

She was right. I did want the best for her and if this situation was reversed I would be acting the same way she is now. We both laughed and changed the subject.

For the rest of the night, we didn't mention Allen or Anthony again and stayed till the pub staff finally kicked us out. I walked Sam back to her place, and we said our goodbyes with tear-filled eyes and had a long hug, knowing this was it till the end of next term. Sam went inside and I headed for home. The night was calm and the sky clear, not a common thing around here this time of year. I looked up at the stars as I walked down the old road back into town for home, and it gave me plenty of time to think and reflect on what I should do. While I still didn't have an answer, I kept playing over Sam's thoughts about it as I rounded the corner for home.

When I approached my door, Allen was sitting on the steps. I was in no mood to see him, but he looked more upset than I had ever seen him. "Allen, are you all right?"

He looked up. "Oh David, yeah, I... This... I... It's late, I'm sorry. I shouldn't have come here and just waited till morning."

I just stared at him for a moment. "Well, you're here now so we might as well talk," I said as I sat down next to him on the stoop.

"I'm sorry for all of this. I was thinking about running into you at the pub with Sam, and I couldn't help but think I ruined your night, and with everything that happened earlier, I just made a mess of this and fucked up everything today."

I leaned my head on his shoulder. "I was glad to see you, and yes, you've given me a lot to think about but it's nice to know where things are with us. Now I need to figure out what's best for me in this situation."

We both just sat there looking up into the sky. We sat this way for about a good fifteen minutes before the porch light came on and Mum was standing at the door.

"Oh David, it's you and Allen. I heard male voices but couldn't see anything. Why don't you two come in? It's getting cold and late out here."

We stood up. "Sorry, Mum, we didn't mean to scare you. I'll be in soon."

She smiled and shut the door. Allen and I just looked at each other. "Well, since I'm in town, why don't we head back to school together in a few days?" Allen said in a shy manner, and I just smiled.

"Yeah, I'd like that. I'll call you tomorrow. I'm sure Mum and Grandma will want to see you before we leave."

He smiled before giving me a kiss on the cheek, then turned around and walked off into the night.

Chapter 20
A PERFECT DAY

The following day, my mind was racing, and I was starting to feel panic overcome me. I was frozen sitting there on my bed when Mum knocked on the door. "David, honey, are you okay?" She entered the room and sat next to me. "I'm sure you're having a lot of mixed feelings right now about Anthony and Allen. I'm here to talk if you want."

I looked at her. "I am so confused I do not know what I should do and what is right Mum. Anthony and I were just starting to get back on track in our relationship, but Allen is the one I'm in love with." I sighed.

Mum put her arm around me. "Well, no one can tell you what to do. I think Allen would be better for you, but that's just my feeling; you have to decide if you and Anthony can continue to grow your relationship. Still, if you think not, it's not every day a guy would fly around the world to tell you he loves you," she said with a tone of *get it through your thick skull, you idiot,* and a wide smile.

I gave her a small fake half-smile. I knew she was right; I had to figure it out myself. "Thanks, Mum," I said. With that, she kissed my head, got up, and walked out of the room.

I was planning to spend the day helping Grandma and Grandad around the farm. I told Allen last night that I was sure Grandma would like to see him, so I texted him to see if he wanted to come along. He responded within seconds like he was just sitting there waiting for my text or call.

We had so much fun last time, I cannot wait. I'll meet you at the road leading to the farm.

I put my phone into my pocket, grabbed my jumper, and headed down the stairs. Mum and Dad were sitting in the parlor when I came down, Dad looking up from over his paper. "Good morning, David. What are your plans for today?" He grinned at me knowingly, so I guessed Mum told him Allen was in town.

"I promised Grandma and Grandad that I would help out on the farm today before I head back to university tomorrow."

"Oh I see, and are we to expect any more unplanned visitors while you're away?" He laughed, and Mum hit him on the arm.

"Oh, leave the boy alone, he's just doing what we always wanted for him—to go out and have a fun life."

Dad looked at her. "I was only joking with him; he knows that, don't you, David."

I smiled at both of them. "Yeah, I know. Well, I best be off, you know how Grandad gets if I'm late." With that Dad grunted and went back to his paper and I headed out the door.

The sun was bright today and the weather was nice. The village was active with people moving in all directions getting to work or opening their shops. I made my way down to the path leading up to my grandparents' farm and there under the only tree on the entire road was Allen waiting for me as promised. We headed up the winding way together and made small talk, neither one of us wanting to bring up last night.

Once we made it to the farm, Grandma was waiting on the porch for my arrival. "Oh David, sweetie, it's so good to see you, and oh, you brought Allen with you this time. What happened to the other boy, um...what's his name."

I smiled and gave her a hug and a kiss on the cheek. "His name is Anthony, Grandma, and he went back to America. Allen and I are traveling back tomorrow together since he was in Europe on holiday."

She smiled and hugged Allen. "Oh yes, of course I knew that. Well, your grandad is out in the barn getting the horses ready. I'm sure he'll be glad to have the extra pair of hands. Off you go now, the day's wasted sitting here with me."

With that Allen and I turned and headed off the porch and to the barn.

When we arrived, Grandad was coming out with two horses saddled and ready to go. When he looked up and saw that Allen was with me, he said, "Oh, I didn't know you were bringing help. I need to get another horse ready. No matter, you both can take these and head out to the far pasture. Take the dog; we need to get the sheep back to the barn today, there's rain coming."

We each took a horse, climbed on, I called for the dogs, and off we went to the pastures to start rounding up the sheep, Just like last time, I was amazed that Allen was so good at this and we had such a blast running the horses and getting the sheep herded together that by the time Granddad and the rest of his farmhands arrived from the other pastures with their flocks, we were ready to go.

"I'm impressed, boys, usually it takes David all day to get this pasture rounded up. You're one fine farmhand, Allen," Granddad said with a smile on his face, his pipe hanging out of the corner of his mouth. Allen smiled and we all headed back to the barns with our sheep.

Once back, the farmhands took over getting the sheep into the pens, and Allen and I were free to take the horses back to their barn. We led them into their stalls and got them unsaddled, brushed and cleaned, and fed and watered. Allen and I had a nice discussion about horse care, and I was again so amazed at how much he knew that I finally asked him, "How are you so good at this? I'm amazed. You're an arts major, yet you're very athletic, and apparently a master of horses."

Allen laughed. "Oh come on now, David, I still have to have some secrets."

We both laughed and headed out of the barn and back to the house to find Grandma had made us something to eat and was in the middle of setting the table. We helped her finish and the three of us sat down and ate together. It was a fun time; we told stories, and Grandad even joined us later and was laughing and telling stories from my childhood to Allen about how I was so bad at horse riding that compared to him I was that child again. I didn't even care how embarrassing it was, they were all getting along, and this made me start to think that maybe they would be okay with a gay grandson, and maybe they would be okay if I decided not to take over the farm. This day had ended up being perfect, but now I was starting to feel sick. I had to tell Anthony about Allen showing up and everything that happened; I owed it to him if I wanted to make our relationship work. I wasn't sure if I wanted to make it work anymore, but I knew that if I didn't tell him and we did try this would not end well.

After we finished eating and cleaned up, Allen and I said our goodbyes and headed down the road back to the village. Once we made it to my street, we hugged and then Allen told me that he enjoyed today and would be over first thing tomorrow so we could head back to school together. I was afraid that he was going to ask if I'd made up my mind, but thankfully he did not and we went our separate ways. Once home I ran up to my room, dreading what I had to do next.

I sat on my bed, still not knowing what I should do. I kept thinking about what everyone said and their advice; what was I not seeing that they preferred Allen over Anthony? What did they see that I couldn't, and why would they not tell me? I was annoyed with this and grabbed my phone and texted Anthony.

Hey, we need to talk. Allen came by the other day and things got weird.

I knew it was late, but I hoped my mentioning Allen meant he would respond quickly. Minutes passed, and nothing. I put my phone on the bedside table, rolled over, and went to sleep.

The following morning, I woke to see a text from Anthony.

What do you mean he came by? And what do you mean it got weird?

I started to panic. I knew I had to tell him and wanted to, but I was now afraid of how things would go.

He came over and confessed that he was in love with me and wanted to be with me.

I thought it was for the best not to tell him that he kissed me again and that, this time, I kissed him back or that I told him I would think about it. I knew telling him this would be a massive issue, so I waited for his response to come in. Soon, my phone buzzed.

What do you mean he confessed his love to you? Did he actually say he loved you?

My heart was racing.

Yeah, he was standing in my parlor room and told me he'd traveled around the world to tell me that he was in love with me, and he couldn't wait for school to start to tell me.

I was waiting for his blow-up call or text, but when my phone buzzed, it was not what I expected.

I'm sure he's just messing with you. There's no way he was being serious. Allen will go to any lengths to pull a prank, it's not a big deal. I'll see you when I pick you up from the airport. Love you.

I frowned. Maybe he was right. Perhaps it was a joke, but why was he so relaxed that Allen, the one person he hated most in this world, showed up at my house unannounced and professed his love to me? Something seemed off, but I put it out of my mind and started my day.

Chapter 21
RETURN TO SCHOOL

My alarm went off the following day. I rolled over and turned it off. I sat on the edge of my bed. I was feeling the lack of sleep from last night. I stood up, walked into the bathroom, and started the shower. Standing under the hot water felt nice and was the wake-up I needed. I just stood there enjoying the water and heat before I snapped out of it, turned off the water, and started to get ready for the day.

After packing, I headed to the kitchen to find Mum and Dad sitting at the table waiting for me. I made a cup of tea and sat down at the table to join them. We had an excellent traditional breakfast and chatted about this upcoming term, the classes I was taking, and whether I was planning to stay in the summer or come home. I thought it was too early to talk about summer when the semester was only just starting. Mum and Dad tried to push it but I kept blowing it off; I had too much on my mind to worry about the summer holidays. After everything was cleaned up, I headed up to my room, collected my bags, and loaded them into the car. Just as I finished, Allen walked up with his, and we loaded them in with mine before shutting the door.

Dad, Allen, and I started the long drive to the airport. It was quiet. Dad and I didn't say much to one another, and once we made it to the airport, Dad helped us unload our bags and watched as we walked into the airport. Once inside, we went through security and found the gate. Allen had managed to get his flight changed to mine without me knowing. I did what I always do: open a book and bury my nose in it until it was time to board. We boarded the plane, found our seats, and then I returned to my book. The flight was uneventful, and nothing went wrong. When we started our descent into Michigan, I texted Anthony to tell him that I would message him once the plane landed. Allen said that once we landed he had some business to take care of and would come to find me after we were both home and settled. I think he just didn't want to deal with Anthony, and honestly, I didn't want there to be a fight in the middle of the airport so I just agreed.

The plane landed, and once we were off, I texted Anthony to let him know I would soon be down to the baggage claim. I'd begun to head that way when I heard a familiar voice behind me. "David, is that you?" I turned around to see Alessia standing there. I smiled, and she ran up to me and hugged me. "I'm so glad to see you; I missed you and wished you would have come to see me during the holiday. I'm sure you were busy, but we can catch up later. Who's picking you up? Mark is waiting for me in baggage claim."

It was nice to see her, and I could hear her excitement. "Oh, Anthony is picking me up."

She smiled, and we headed off to baggage claim together. When we arrived, I saw Anthony standing there waiting for me. He ran up to me, hugged me, and kissed me. I kissed him back, but it didn't feel the same as the other day when Allen and I kissed. Alessia walked up next to us. Anthony looked at her and smiled. "Oh, Alessia, it's so good to see you. Is Mark here somewhere? Do you need a ride home?"

She smiled back at Anthony. "Hi Anthony, it's great to see you. Mark is here somewhere, most likely over by the bag conveyor."

We all started heading over to the conveyors to wait for our luggage. They began coming down the belt, and once we had mine, Anthony and I went over to Alessia and helped her collect hers. The three of us headed outside, and once out there, we saw Mark. He and Alessia kissed and loaded her bags into his car. We all said our hellos and goodbyes, and then Anthony and I got into his car and headed off to my apartment.

When we returned to the apartment, Anthony and I took my bags into my room. He started unpacking for me, and I went into the kitchen to make some tea. I sat in the kitchen waiting for the kettle to be done, just thinking about when Anthony would address the Allen problem or if we would act like it didn't happen. The tea kettle finished, and I poured two cups and headed back into the bedroom to help Anthony.

Anthony had pretty much everything unpacked and put away already. "Oh wow, you made that look easy," I said in a happy tone.

Anthony gave me a side-eye. "Well, now that's done, we can have some time together just the two of us?" He looked at me wildly. I sat the cups of tea on the side table, and Anthony pushed me onto the bed and jumped on top. We had a fun, passionate time; though while I was enjoying myself, this time it didn't feel the same as other times we had been together. Once finished, we got dressed and headed into the living room.

Anthony sat on the couch smiling while I ordered something to eat, as there was no food in the apartment. I needed to go shopping but was too tired from the trip to go out now. Once our food was ordered, I sat next to him and said, "We need to talk about Allen and what him professing his love means."

Anthony looked at me with a frown. "I don't want to talk about it; can we just pretend it never happened?"

I was getting mad. "NO, we can't act like it didn't happen. Allen is my friend, and I can't just avoid him."

Anthony looked like he was going to explode from hearing me say that. "Why can't you just forget about it and not talk to Allen? I'm not asking for much; we're partners and must be on the same page if this will work."

I frowned. I didn't want to lose Allen, but I also didn't want to lose Anthony. "I'll drop it, but Allen is my friend, and I will not lose our friendship. You have Trevor, which I don't like, and I let you stay in contact with him, so I'm staying in contact with Allen."

Anthony looked like he would still explode, but then he said, "Fine...you can be friends with him, but I don't want to hear more about him and his apparent love for you."

I smiled at this; I knew he had just compromised for me, and this made me feel good.

Moments later, the doorbell rang. I answered, collected our food, and shut the door. I walked back over to the couch, and Anthony and I ate and chatted about our upcoming classes and plans for the rest of the week before classes started. Things were going well until I mentioned that we had dinner with Mark, Alessia, and Allen tonight. He looked like he was going to be sick. "Oh, well, I don't think I'm coming to dinner tonight."

Confused, I looked at him. "What do you mean you're not coming tonight? Everyone is expecting all of us to be together again."

Anthony frowned. "I just don't think I can be in the same room as Allen right now, and after the way the last dinner with all of us went, I don't think it would be wise." He looked at his watch. "I have to get going anyway; I have to return the car." With that, he stood up, collected his coat, and walked out. I just sat there on the couch, confused and upset. I cleaned up our food and headed to my room to shower.

Standing in the shower with the water running, I couldn't help thinking about how Anthony was being so unreasonable about dinner tonight, why he was so quick to shut it down, and why he ran out so fast. I knew he had to return the car, but it was clear that he was using it as an excuse to get out of the conversation. I decided not to think about it anymore and finished my shower, then started to get ready for dinner, hoping Anthony would change his mind.

Once I was dressed, I decided to text him to get him to reconsider.

Hey, I would really like it if you came tonight. I know you think it'll be awkward, but I want the whole friend group together.

Soon, my phone buzzed.

I know you want to spend time together, and dinner would be nice with our friends, but I don't want to see Allen. Maybe just the four of us could go out one night when Allen is busy. I'm sorry, but I don't want to be in the same room as him.

I was aggravated that he was being so unreasonable. Still, I was too tired and didn't want to fight, so I dropped it and threw my phone down. I wondered how I was going to explain to Alessia, Mark, and Allen that Anthony didn't want to come tonight and not make a big deal out of it.

Chapter 22
DINNER WITH FRIENDS

The time had come to head out to the restaurant for dinner. I had not heard from Alessia and Mark since the airport. I was sure they had been busy catching up and doing other things, but I was surprised that I still had not heard from Allen. I figured I would see him at dinner. I was excited to see him, but also I had to remember that he wanted to act as if nothing had happened. I was still conflicted by that, but deep down I knew that it was for the best to keep the peace between everyone. I grabbed my coat and headed out to the lobby. There, I saw Mark and Alessia heading out the door. I caught up to them, and the three of us started to walk to the restaurant. I asked if anyone had heard from Allen, and no one had; then Mark asked where Anthony was. I explained that he was not coming for some reason and left it at that. Mark didn't pry into it, and we all continued walking to the restaurant in silence.

Once at the restaurant, we met with Allen, who was waiting for us. I smiled once I saw him, and he smiled back when he saw me looking at him. We updated him that Anthony was not coming, and we let the hostess know we were all there and ready to be seated. We were taken to our table, and once settled, we all ordered drinks and food and started to talk about various trips and what our upcoming semesters looked like. Our food arrived, and we all started eating. The night was going very well, but deep down, I was feeling anger at Anthony for not wanting to come, and also anxiety that I knew eventually Allen and I would have to have the conversation about us and me deciding that it would be best to stay with Anthony. I hoped we could still be friends. The more I thought about this, the more I started feeling sick. I stopped eating and just sat there. It wasn't long before the others noticed.

Alessia was the first to speak. "David? Are you okay?"

I looked up from my plate. "Yeah, I'm fine. I was just deep in thought for a second there."

They all just looked at me intently. Allen then spoke. "Are you sure, David? I don't think we've ever seen you that zoned out."

I smiled at their concern. "I'm fine, guys, really promise, I was just lost in thought about the upcoming semester."

They seemed to accept this, and we returned to our conversation and dinner.

We continued our meals, chatting, and were finishing our drinks when the waiter approached the table. "So, how was everything tonight?" he asked with a pleasant demeanor. We all let him know everything was delicious. "Can I get anyone anything else or some dessert?"

The three of them cheered for dessert, but I still felt sick and declined. They ordered their desserts, and I asked for my bill. The waiter took their orders and headed off. When he came back, he set their food down, then placed a piece of cake in front of me along with my bill, and winked before he walked off. I was confused, and when I picked up the bill there was no charge for the cake. There was a note—*call me sometime*—and his number. I smiled and put it in my pocket. I didn't want to think about someone else when Allen was sitting across from me and with Anthony and me trying to work on things. We all ate our desserts, the waiter brought over their bills, we all paid, and then we started to get ready to head out.

While walking out, I excused myself to the restroom and then ran straight into our waiter. "Oh hey," he said in an upbeat tone.

"Oh, hi. Thanks for the cake; it was really nice of you to give me that. I've been having a bad day so it was a nice pick-me-up."

"Oh, it was nothing. I could tell you were not really into everyone and their conversations tonight. I'm Michael."

He gave me a soft smile, and I smiled back. "Nice to meet you. I'm David."

We just sat there smiling at each other a little longer.

"Well, I better get going before my friends start to worry about me. I have your number, so I'll text you sometime."

On my way to the table, I thought, what the hell was I thinking, saying I would text him sometime? Why was I so stupid? I tried to put it out of my mind.

The four of us walked back to our apartment building. Alessia and Mark kept talking about the cute waiter and how he was clearly sweet on me. I smiled but kept blowing them off. I could tell that Allen was not too thrilled with them bringing it up, and I didn't want to make it any more awkward, knowing our conversation about us was coming up. It was going to be hard already.

Once back in the lobby of our building, Mark and Alessia said goodbye to Allen and me and headed off for her apartment. Allen and I sat down in the lobby and chatted about dinner and how funny it was that the waiter gave me his number with the cake so I would text him. I thought to myself how it was actually sweet and good that Allen and I could laugh about it, and then he finally asked, "So what's the real reason Anthony didn't come tonight?"

I thought, *Great, here comes our conversation. He wants to know if he didn't come because I called it off.* I smiled at him. "Well, to be honest, I did tell him about you coming to my house and professing your love for me, and he didn't take it well, as expected; he told me that he doesn't want to be in the same room as you, and I told him that I wouldn't let our friendship end over him not wanting to be around you, so he didn't come."

Allen frowned and looked at me sadly. "Friendship, huh? So does that mean you're turning me down?"

My stomach started flipping. "No, I'm not turning you down; I just think I need to give Anthony and me a chance. I also have feelings for you. I just think we had bad timing on being honest with each other about our feelings."

Again, he frowned and looked down at the ground.

I continued, "I care greatly for you, Allen, and I don't want what we have to end, but if I were to leave Anthony, I would be no better than him."

He looked up with a smile on his face. "You're right, David, that's why I love you; no matter what, you're loyal and do what's best for everyone."

With that, we stood up and walked to our apartments.

Back in my apartment, I couldn't help thinking about how the day had gone so far: Anthony and I not being able to see eye to eye, and him refusing to come to dinner with all of our friends, then the waiter being sweet on me and giving me his number, then me being stupid and telling him I would text him sometime. Lastly, I'd made Allen feel bad, and that was bothering me most of all; I never wanted to hurt him. All I ever wanted was to be with him, but I never thought it would be possible. Why did he have to tell me he loved me? Why couldn't he keep his feelings a secret from me like I did with him? I decided I had to talk to him. I had to let him know how he had complicated things for me, and I was so confused and upset that he couldn't have confessed his feelings and love for me when we were on our vacation in Europe together. I walked out of my apartment and up the stairs to his floor. I could hear him playing his cello with a passion I had not yet heard from him. I had heard him play now on two different occasions, and he was also so reserved and perfect this time that the hall was filling with his music. I could feel he was putting his emotions into the music. I recognized the song as the one he had played at the concert we all went to, but this time, his "I'll Never Love Again" was different; you could hear and feel the hurt in it. I made it to his door and just listened. I didn't want to knock as I didn't want his playing to stop. I loved his playing, and I could feel his pain. It made me feel sad for him.

Once his playing stopped, I knocked. I heard him put his cello down and walk over to the door. When he opened it, he looked surprised to see me. "Oh, David? Are you okay? Please come in."

I walked in. "That was beautiful, Allen. I could feel your emotions in your playing; why don't you play like that in public?"

He smiled as he packed his cello into the case. "I play how I feel; I guess when I'm in public, I let my nerves take hold and focus on perfection over emotion." Once he had the cello packed away, he turned to me. "So, what's up? I don't think you came here to hear me play and tell me you liked it."

I frowned. "Well, you're right, I didn't. I came here as I've been thinking... Why did you wait so long to confess your feelings for me? Why did you wait until Anthony and I were better to say something? We spent a whole week in Europe together, why didn't you say anything then?"

Allen had a sad look on his face. "You think I didn't try? David, I took you to meet my Aunt Vi, and I know she told you that was something special. I also surprised you with a performance of my feelings not once but twice. Jesus, David, can you be so dense that you couldn't have seen what I was doing?" His sadness was now looking like anger. I didn't know what to say. Then he said, "I thought we had such a romantic holiday together in Europe, first London and my performance, then at your village and seeing all the sights and sounds together, the boating trip to the isle." His tone was growing more and more serious. "I even flew around the world after I realized it wasn't setting in for you and professed my love for you in person in front of you and with your mother sitting in the kitchen. Anthony hasn't done anything like that for you, and yet I'm pushed to the side for him. I don't get it, David. What is it that you want in life, when someone is standing in front of you who is the one for you and you still stay in your toxic relationship and then flirt with the waiter in front of that same person as well and promise to text him? Yeah, I saw you two talking, and when I heard that I walked away before you saw me. I was hoping you would have mentioned it when we were talking in the lobby. I will always love you, David, but you've made it clear I'm not the one you want, and for me as someone who struggles with his sexuality, as well as other issues that I don't want to get into right now, that was a massive step for me to do what I did, thinking there was any chance for us. I'm sorry but I can't do this right now. Please leave."

I was frozen in shock at what I had just heard. I didn't know how to respond; I just told him he was right and walked out of his apartment.

Once in the hall, I could hear him throw what sounded like a lamp, and I just said to myself out loud, "David, you idiot, you just ruined not only your chance at a perfect relationship but also your friendship." Tears started to run down my face, and I walked down to my floor. I made it to my place now in a full-on ugly cry, when I saw Alessia and Mark come out of her apartment. She saw me crying, and before I could make it through my door she was hugging me and asking what was wrong. "I fucked everything up. I just ruined mine and Allen's relationship, and I don't think there's any way to fix it."

She hugged me tightly. Mark excused himself to check on Allen, and I kept crying into Alessia's shoulder while she tried to comfort me. "Oh, David, what happened, honey?" she said with such a sweet tone. We went inside and sat on the couch, and I told her everything that happened between me and Allen, still crying. She looked at me. "Oh, David honey, he's hurt, and I'm sure he'll come around to the fact that he should have been more straightforward with you about his feelings and that it's hard for you to pick up on when someone has feelings for you. As for the waiter, I'm sure you were just being the nice sweet David that you are." I smiled at her, tears still in my eyes, but I felt better. We sat there chatting about anything to keep my mind off things while waiting for Mark to return.

Mark returned after what felt like hours but was really only about twenty minutes. When he entered my apartment, I stood up quickly and asked, "How is he? Is he all right?"

Mark raised his hand to calm me. "He's fine; he's hurt, but he's okay. Can't say the same for his lamp, but he didn't hurt himself, and that's what's important. Give him some time to come around, okay?"

I frowned at this but knew he was right. Mark and Alessia said their goodbyes and headed out. I took a shower and headed to bed, and it didn't take me long to fall asleep from the day's events.

Chapter 23
MICHAEL

Three days had passed since the dinner, and I had not heard from Allen. Anthony was still mad that I went to the dinner and was being short whenever we talked. I was starting to think I had made a massive mistake, but I didn't know what to do. Sitting in my apartment, I was feeling sad and lonely. I don't know what came over me, but I found the check with Michael's number and texted him.

Hi Michael, it's David from the restaurant the other night. I just wanted to thank you again for the dessert; it was lovely.

As soon as I sent it, I instantly panicked and regretted it. My phone buzzed almost immediately.

Hey David, I'm glad you texted. I was starting to think that maybe you weren't interested. I'm glad my offering gave you a nice pick-me-up. I was wondering if we could get a coffee sometime as friends?

I smiled; there was no harm in being friends. I texted him back.

That sounds nice. I would love to get a coffee with a friend.

We texted back and forth some more and set a coffee date for later in the day. I was looking forward to getting out of the apartment; being in a depressed state for the past three days was taking a toll on me, and this would be good for me, I thought to myself as I started to get out of bed and head to the shower to get ready for my outing later.

The time had come to head for the cafe. On my way down to the lobby, I ran into Alessia in the elevator. "David, it's so good to see you out. How are you doing?"

I smiled. "I'm well; I'm just on my way out to get a coffee with a friend."

She looked at me as if trying to read if I was being truthful. "Well, that sounds lovely. I'm glad you're coming out of the funk you've been in these past few days."

Once in the lobby, we said our goodbyes and headed in different directions.

The walk to the cafe was uneventful, with many people walking in all directions wearing heavy coats as the day was frigid and it had snowed the night before. Many of the grounds had yet to be shoveled, so doing my best to keep my balance, I made my way slowly to the cafe. When I arrived there, I saw Michael inside sitting at a table. I entered, waved at him, and approached the line of people waiting to place their coffee orders. When at the front of the line, I gave my order and waited for my coffee to be ready, then I walked over to the table Michael was sitting at and sat down. "Hi," I said in a cheery tone.

He smiled. "Hi, David, it's good to see you."

We chatted and laughed about life and anything else we could think of, and things were going very well. I was feeling better about everything that had happened just at the moment Anthony walked into the cafe. I started to feel sick. I wasn't doing anything wrong, but I didn't want to be seen with Michael, knowing that Anthony would not handle it well.

I sat still, hoping he didn't see me and trying not to make it apparent to Michael that I was uncomfortable and why that was. Michael excused himself to the restroom; I took this moment to go over to Anthony so that he didn't see me with Michael. I grabbed him from behind and kissed his cheek. Anthony turned around in a panic, but once he saw it was me, he smiled. "Oh David, what are you doing here?"

I smiled. "Oh, a friend and I are just getting a coffee and catching up about life and whatnot. What are you doing?"

He smiled back at me. "Oh, that sounds nice. I'm just on my way to a meeting for class and stopped for something warm to drink to help with this cold. What are you doing later tonight? Maybe we can have dinner together?"

I smiled. "That sounds good. Come over at 6:00 pm tonight, and I'll cook for us." We kissed each other goodbye, and Anthony turned and headed out of the cafe; with that, I made my way back to the table as Michael was coming out of the restroom.

"Who was that guy you were talking to?" Michael asked with a smile on his face, but also with an undertone of and do not lie about it.

"Oh, that was my boyfriend, Anthony," I said quickly.

Michael looked at me, and his smile grew more prominent. "Oh, boyfriend, huh? That's nice, now I feel stupid."

I frowned. "Please don't. I've enjoyed our talk and would like to be friends," I said in a way that I hoped showed him I was for real.

Michael gave a half smile. "I've enjoyed this too, and I would like to be friends. Maybe next time, the three of us can all hang out together," he said.

We continued to chat about things and drink our coffee, and everything was going well before it was time to say our goodbyes and head out. As we were walking out the door, Michael told me he'd had a great time and then went in for a hug, which I returned, and as we were letting go, he kissed me on the cheek. This took me aback, and we walked off out the door.

Walking back to my apartment, I was in deep thought about what had just happened and tried to overcome my confusion. Michael knew about Anthony now. He knew this was just a friendly date, and he even offered to hang out with the three of us, so why in the hell would he still kiss me even if it was just on the cheek? I eventually decided it was harmless and not to let it take up any more space in my mind. Once I had made it back to my building, I collected my mail from the mailbox and then headed up to my flat to start prepping for my dinner tonight with Anthony.

Around 5:30, I put the dinner in the oven so that it would be done around 6:00 when Anthony arrived. I was sitting there at the table, not having anything to do, when my phone buzzed. I looked at it, thinking maybe it was Anthony, but it was Michael.

Hey David, today was great. I wish I could have met your boyfriend while he was there, maybe next time, also I hope the kiss didn't weird you out. I couldn't help myself.

I just smiled and put my phone back down. I wasn't sure how to respond and didn't want to anyway. I figured I would bring it up to Anthony to ensure he knew I wasn't hiding anything from him.

Chapter 24
DINNER WITH ANTHONY

Dinner was almost done, and I was setting the table when I heard a knock at the door. I put the plates down to answer, figuring it had to be Anthony. I walked over and opened the door. To my surprise, Allen stood there. "Hey David, I just wanted to check in on you and see how you've been?"

I smiled, seeing he still cared. "I'm fine, thanks for asking. I'm just getting ready for dinner with Anthony; he should be here soon." Allen frowned at this. I changed the subject, and we chatted more about things. We were so busy conversing that neither of us saw Anthony come off the elevator. I saw him over Allen's shoulder as he walked up with a look of distaste. "Anthony, hey," I said in a cheerful tone. The look of horror on Allen's face was almost funny enough to laugh, but I withheld.

Allen turned around quickly. "Oh hey, Anthony, I was just checking in and will now leave you two to enjoy your evening." He gave a half smile and ran off.

Anthony just looked at me, and I let him in.

Once inside, I led Anthony to the table and went and pulled our dinner out of the oven and put it on the table. I sat down across from Anthony and waited for him to talk; it didn't take long. "Soooo...what did Allen want?"

I smiled at him, knowing this was a simple thing and that there was nothing to worry about. "Oh, he just stopped by to say hi. I told him I was cooking dinner for us, and we just talked in the hall."

Anthony smiled at this and did not pry further. We chatted more about his day after seeing him earlier and how his meeting had ended. Everything was going well, but I had this feeling in the pit of my stomach; I wasn't sure if it was about Allen and Anthony seeing one another or if it was about Michael.

Our dinner was still going well, so I tried not to let the feeling overwhelm me. Eventually, we started to run out of things to discuss, so I decided this was the perfect moment to tell him about my meeting with Michael today. "So the friend I was with today at the cafe said he would like to meet you sometime and that the three of us should hang out."

Anthony looked up from his plate. "Oh yeah, that sounds nice. Maybe we can start having a group of friends, just the two of us, that doesn't revolve around Allen, Alessia, and Mark."

I was annoyed by his comment but figured once I told him how we met and about him kissing my cheek after I told him I was in a relationship, he wouldn't feel the same, and maybe he would see Allen as not so bad. "Well, I need to tell you that I met him when I was out to dinner the other night; he was the waiter at the restaurant and gave me his number. When I was with him today, I ensured he understood that I was in a relationship and looking for friendship only, but he kissed me on the cheek when we were leaving the cafe." I thought it best not to tell him about the text just before he arrived.

Anthony just stared at me; he didn't seem mad or like he was about to explode like I expected him to. Eventually, he opened his mouth to speak. "Hmmm, well...I'm glad you told me, and maybe we have to be cautious around this friend."

I was shocked by his reaction; this was not the Anthony I knew. Where was the rage? Where was the making me feel bad? Why was he so relaxed about this guy I had just met kissing me? Had this been Allen, he would have lost his mind. The more I thought about it, the more I started to worry maybe something was up with him; maybe he was talking to Trevor, or perhaps he was seeing someone around here. My stomach was in a full knot, and I felt like I was going to puke. I settled my stomach and finished my dinner.

Once dinner was finished, I cleared the plates and started a pot of tea, and we moved into the living room, where we sat on the couch and chatted some more. Anthony tried to lean in and kiss me, but I was still in my feelings, so I pulled away. I could see on his face that he was upset about this, but I didn't care. We watched TV and talked about classes and life before the hour ran well into the morning. I was tired now, but I didn't feel right having him walk home, so I offered for him to stay, and we both headed to the bedroom.

In bed, I rolled over, and he cuddled up next to me. It didn't feel right; there was no connection between us, and I was starting to wonder if I had made a mistake by staying with him and then burning bridges with Allen by calling him out. I just lay there, unable to sleep. My mind was racing. Everything was still wrong, things hadn't gone as I had hoped. I had no idea what to do, and it was making me feel worse than I had been feeling the past few days. I finally drifted off to sleep.

When morning came, I woke to find Anthony had already gotten up, and I could hear the shower running. I managed to get out of bed and headed to the kitchen to start the kettle and make breakfast for us. A few minutes later, Anthony came out into the living room with just his towel around his waist. "Good morning," I said with a devious smile on my face at the sight of him.

"Good morning, David," he said back in a monotone.

"I'm just about done with breakfast, so why don't you go put some clothes on and join me?" I looked at him and waited for any kind of response, he just smiled and dropped his towel so I could see him in all his glory before he turned around, walked back to the room, and returned with some pants on.

We sat down at the table and started to eat our breakfast. We sat there in silence, neither one of us wanting to make the first move on starting the conversation about how odd things were between us and what we were going to do to get things back on track in our relationship, or what to do about this new potential friend Michael and his inability to understand that we were in a relationship and not looking for more than just a friend. Finally, I decided to address the Michael situation. "So this Michael guy, what should we do about him?" I looked at him with a pleasant smile on my face to show him I was serious about wanting his input.

Anthony looked up from his plate and smiled at me. "Well, I think maybe we should hang out with him together, make it clear that you and I are in a serious relationship and that if he wants to be friends with you or us, that he understands it's strictly platonic and nothing more."

I was happy that he was willing to talk about this and had a valid response. "I agree with you that we should give him a chance, and I think the three of us hanging out is a great idea."

We finished our breakfast and cleaned up, then went back into the bedroom. I headed into the shower while he finished getting dressed, and once out, I got ready and we headed out the door to start our days. We walked down to the lobby together, and once out the door, we kissed each other goodbye, and I walked off towards the stores and shops. He walked the other way towards his apartment.

Chapter 25
UNEXPECTED NIGHT

I spent the morning at the shops getting the things I needed for school and doing some food shopping. Walking with my bags down the street towards my apartment, I heard a voice behind me. "Oh, David, it's nice to see you," Michael said as he approached me.

"Oh Michael, hey, it's nice to see you too. How are things?"

We chatted briefly, and Michael walked with me back to my place. We were talking pleasantly in the lobby when Anthony called. I excused myself and took his call. "Hey Anthony, how are you?"

I could hear an upbeat tone when he responded, "Oh, I'm great, just getting things done. It just came to my mind; maybe we shouldn't hang out with Michael. I don't know why; I just have this odd feeling."

I didn't want to tell him that Michael was with me, so I just told him we could talk about it later, and he hung up. After I put my phone away, I walked back over to Michael. "Well, thanks for walking with me and chatting, but I really need to get this stuff up to my place and put it away."

He stared at me briefly, then said, "Oh, yeah... Well, I could help you if you want."

I smiled. "That's all right, I'll manage, but we should hang out again soon and maybe Anthony will join us."

He just smiled, we said our goodbyes, and he left the lobby; once he was out of sight, I turned to the elevator and headed up to my apartment. I set the bags on the counter and thought about what happened. Michael clearly wanted to have some kind of relationship, and at first, Anthony was okay with the idea; now he wasn't and was once again making it difficult for me to have any friends. First Allen and now Michael. What was I going to do about it? I started to put the food into the fridge and was running the whole mess over and over in my head. I wanted to talk to someone, but who could I talk to? I didn't want to bring Sam into this, and I also didn't want to put Alessia in the middle again. That only left Allen, and there was no way I was going to ask him about Anthony or Michael, not after our fight. I wasn't going to hurt him any more than I already had.

I texted Sam.

Hey, so Anthony was okay with me making a friend and the three of us hanging out together, but now he's changed his mind. What do you think that's all about?

I continued to put away the shopping while I waited for her to respond to me. Eventually, after everything was packed away, Sam replied.

Hey David, I would say he's just worried about another Allen situation. Maybe the three of you can do lunch in a local place and see how they hit it off?

We texted back and forth a bit about how life was going for both of us before we said our goodbyes. I sat down to eat something and decide what I should do about the Michael and Anthony situation; I even spent some time thinking about what I should do about Allen. We hadn't spoken since that night, and when I saw him in the lobby the other day, he made a point to steer clear of me. That hurt. I knew that I had hurt him, but to completely avoid me and pretend that we didn't exist to one another just seemed so extreme.

I decided I would make things right as best I could, so I wrote him a note detailing how sorry I was for hurting him, and how I hoped we could at least acknowledge one another when we crossed paths and hopefully build some kind of relationship from the ashes of this mess. Once I finished it I ran up to his floor and stuck it under his door. I then stood there for a second quietly waiting to hear if he was home. After a few minutes, I started to head back down the hall to the elevator when it opened and Allen walked off. "Oh, Allen, hey," I said quickly before he could get around me.

"What are you doing here, David? Haven't you done enough already?" he said in a firm tone that made me feel small.

"Oh I just wanted to check in on you, but you weren't home. I can see you're busy so I'll just get going." And with that I jumped onto the elevator and went back down to my floor before things became any more awkward, as it was very clear Allen was still pissed at me.

Back in my apartment, my heart was pounding so fast I felt it was about to jump out of my chest and land on the floor. I sat on the couch and put my head between my legs just as the room started to spin. I felt like I needed to throw up but nothing was coming up. I had never had this bad of a panic attack before and was honestly getting scared. My mind was racing; why was my run-in with Allen making me feel this way? What was I scared of? I was the one who wanted to see him and took the chance so why did I feel so bad? I could not get my mind to calm or my heart to stop beating out of my chest. I ended up finally getting myself composed enough to make it to the bathroom, where I stripped down, climbed into the shower, and just let the water run over me until this all stopped. About an hour later I finally started to calm down enough that I got out of the shower and dressed, then decided I should text Anthony and see if he would come over so I wasn't alone in case I had another panic attack.

Hey, do you wanna come and spend the night with me again? We can order takeout and watch movies and cuddle on the couch.

He responded a few minutes later. *Yeah, that sounds fun. I'll come back over after I finish some things I need to get done.*

I smiled, sat my phone down, and made myself a cup of tea.

A few hours later I was sitting on the couch watching TV, waiting for Anthony to get here, when I heard a knock on the door. I decided I should surprise him in a fun way, so I ran into the bedroom took off all my clothes, and put on a robe that was barely tied and would fall open with the slightest movement. I ran to the door ready to give Anthony his surprise. I pulled the door open and said, "Hey, sexy, took you long enough."

Seconds later I was in shock. Standing in my doorway was not Anthony but Michael. I quickly made sure that my robe was fully closed while stammering, "Oh, Michael, I am so sorry, I thought you were Anthony. What are you doing here?"

He smiled a very wicked grin. "Well, I can't say I was disappointed by the hello. It's not every day that someone answers the door almost naked and calls me sexy. But anyway, I just wanted to stop by and see if you were okay. You just seemed off today when we ran into each other."

I smiled at how sweet it was that he wanted to check in on someone he hardly knew. It reminded me of how sweet Allen was before he started hating me. "I'm fine, thanks for checking in. I would invite you in but as you can see, or almost saw, I'm expecting to have a fun time once Anthony gets here."

He grinned again. "Oh I can tell, looks like Anthony is in for a super fun time."

We both laughed just as the elevator door opened and Anthony entered into the hall.

"Oh, David, I thought it was going to be just us tonight?"

Michael was quick to respond. "Oh, I was just stopping by to check on David. We ran into each other today when he was shopping and he seemed down so I was just checking in. He already told me he was fine and that he was waiting for you to come over, so I'll just be heading out."

To my surprise, Anthony chimed in, "Oh no, please join us; it was nice of you to stop by and check in on my David, plus it'll be more fun for the three of us." Anthony shot me a sidelong smile that made me feel uneasy.

"Oh, I don't want to impose on you two. I'm sure David was looking for a more special night with you alone," Michael said, trying to not make things awkward.

I chimed in, "No it's fine, please join us. It'll be fun for the three of us to watch awful movies and eat a bunch of junk food."

Michael, seeing that I was okay with him staying, smiled and I let them both in. Once inside I ran back to my room to put my clothes back on. I felt so stupid and just wanted to get through this night without any more embarrassment.

I tried to get dressed as quickly as I could as I didn't want to leave Anthony and Michael alone for long; who knew what they would say to each other and I couldn't handle another fight between any of the people in my life. Once I had my pants on, I turned around to see Anthony standing in the doorway. I jumped at the sight of him. "Jeez, Anthony, you scared the shit out of me. How long have you been standing there?"

Anthony smiled. "Oh, long enough to see that cute little ass of yours."

We both laughed, then I said, "Hey, I'm sorry about Michael being here. I had no clue he would stop by, and I know you're not keen on the idea of being friends with him. I can send him away if you want, I'm sure he'll understand." I felt bad thinking about making him leave but I didn't want to make Anthony more upset than he already had been lately. I looked at him, waiting for him to respond, but he just kept standing there staring and not doing anything. I was getting to the point of worry and feeling sick in my stomach, then he finally spoke.

"No, it's okay. I've been thinking you're right; we could use some friends outside of Allen and Alessia, so let's see how tonight goes. If things go well then we can be friends, and if not we can talk about it."

I smiled and hugged him. "Oh my god, Anthony, thank you."

He hugged me tight and we returned to the main room to get this movie night going.

The three of us sat and talked while we waited for all the food we ordered to arrive. We couldn't decide on what to get so we ended up ordering all of it: pizza, tacos, Chinese, and sushi. We were making bets on what would get here first and so far were having a good time. Anthony and Michael seemed to be getting along and I was starting to settle down and feel less anxious about this whole situation and was glad that since this happened I didn't have to have the conversation with Anthony about giving Michael a chance.

There was a knock on the door, and I got up to answer and see who the winner was for our bet. I opened the door and it was our tacos. I took the food and closed the door, and as I walked back to the couch, I said, "We have tacos. Who said they would get here first?" We all sighed; none of us thought the tacos would be first. I continued, "Well I guess we all lose."

Michael then got a wicked look on his face. "Well, there are three deliveries left. Why don't we each choose one and the last one is the loser and has to do something the winners say."

I started to panic and looked over at Anthony, waiting for him to explode on him. But he didn't. Instead, he said, "Oh my god, that would be hilarious. I pick pizza, you two losers can pick from the others." Michael took the Chinese so I was left with the sushi.

The second order to arrive was the pizza, and Anthony was excited. Now it was down to the wire. I didn't want to lose, and I didn't want to do something that Anthony and Michael came up with; who knew what they would suggest and I was afraid that it would cause a fight. There was a knock on the door. My heart sank, and all three of us answered the door. To my surprise, both delivery guys were there. The three of us cheered, and then I said, "So it's a tie, that means no one loses, right?"

The three of us started laughing, and while the poor delivery guys looked confused, we took the food from them and closed the door. We all walked back to the couch laughing and joking about what must have been going through the delivery guys' minds seeing us open the door and then cheering.

Michael started to speak. "So, Anthony, seems like you won, and David and I lost. I guess that means you get to decide something the both of us have to do."

Anthony got a wicked smile on his face, and I started to feel anxious again. "Well, I'm going to have to think of a punishment for the two of you, but I promise it'll be a great laugh." Michael smiled and they both laughed. I just sat there in my silent panic, fearing what Anthony's "punishment" would be.

We started eating our food. There was so much that I didn't think we would be able to finish it all. Then Anthony started this B-rated horror movie about college students on a road trip—one of those typical slasher films where you know what's gonna happen and can't stand that the characters make horrible choices like running into the basement instead of running outside and getting in the car and driving the hell out of there. We watched a few of these awful movies before I started to fall asleep on Anthony's shoulder.

"You still awake there, David?" he asked while putting his arm around me.

"Yeah, I'm still up." I smiled and looked up at him.

"Well don't go passing out on me; you and Michael still owe me your punishment for losing."

I just smiled and put my head back on his shoulder and continued watching the movie. I must have fallen asleep, as when I opened my eyes there was a new movie on the TV and all of the food mess had been cleaned up. I sat up and looked around. Anthony was sitting next to me but I didn't see Michael. "Oh hey, I guess I fell asleep. Did Michael leave?"

Anthony looked at me. "I wondered if you planned on waking up anytime soon. He's still here, just went to the restroom." A few minutes later Michael reappeared and sat back down in the armchair. We were all sitting there quietly, just watching the movie. The glow from the screen was the only thing giving any light to the room, and there was not a sound around except for the movie. It seemed oddly quiet; usually, you could hear someone in the hall or noise from the street below, but not tonight. It made me feel a little uneasy like something bad was about to happen.

Once the movie had finished, Anthony stood up and I assumed he was going to finally call it a night. I was ready to go back to sleep and was hoping he was going to call it, but then he started to speak. "Well, gentlemen, it's getting late, so I think now is a good time for you two to pay up on our bet."

My stomach started to jump. I had hoped he had forgotten or was just going to let it go but I guess not. I just smiled and Michael did the same before Anthony continued, "David, you'll get yours later, but as for Michael, you have to tell the truth about why you're truly here and what your true intentions are for wanting to be friends with David."

Oh shit, I thought to myself, why did he have to do this now? And if he had such an issue with Michael being here, why was he so persistent that he stayed when Michael and I tried so hard earlier to let him not be a third wheel? My mind was racing and the room was starting to slowly spin. I just hoped that Michael's response wouldn't send Anthony into a rage.

Michael sat there for a few minutes, looking like he was playing over in his head all the ways this could end and how he should maneuver this question of Anthony's. He stood from his chair and took a step back from Anthony, then said, "If you must know the truth, then fine. The truth is that I find David to be a very attractive man, not just because of his looks but his genuine personality as well, something you clearly don't have in common. When he told me he had a boyfriend I respected that and figured, well, maybe we could still be friends. I could tell this made David uneasy and I couldn't figure out why—till now that is. You're a controlling, toxic person and David deserves much better. As to my intentions, it's to show David that there are better guys out there, that he shouldn't settle for just anyone."

I thought what Michael said was sweet and I knew there were others out there; after all, there was Allen and now apparently Michael, but the thought was short-lived as I was now in full fear of Anthony and the fight that was about to ensue.

The rage that came over Anthony's face I had seen before and knew this was going to be bad. He started screaming and calling Michael all kinds of names and insults before turning his attention to me and blaming me for all of this, that it was my fault, I couldn't be happy with how things were between us. I was feeling smaller and smaller by the second, my heart was racing, my stomach was tumbling like it was trying to win a gold medal at the Olympics, and, worse, the room was spinning faster and faster. I needed to escape. When Anthony directed his rage back to Michael, I took my chance and ran out of the apartment.

Once in the hall I didn't know what to do. It was late, I didn't have my phone, and I wasn't about to bring Alessia and Mark into this. I don't know what possessed me but I ran up the stairs to Allen's door and started to knock as hard as I could.

Moments later Allen swung the door open. "Who the hell—?" He saw me and got a look of confusion on his face. "Oh my god, seriously David, what in the hell do you want?"

Everything was moving so fast that I was having trouble trying to put words together. "I... I... I just... I need..." The world started to move in slow motion, and then everything went dark.

Chapter 26
TRUE FRIENDS

I awoke to find myself in a hospital bed. Allen was sleeping on a chair over in the corner, and Michael was sitting by the side of my bed. There was no sign of Anthony anywhere or that he had even been here. I looked around the room for a few more minutes before Michael noticed I was awake. "Oh hey, you're up," he said with a big smile on his face. His loud voice must have startled Allen as I heard him huffing and grunting as he woke up.

I continued to look around the room some more before I started to speak. "Umm, what's going on? Why am I here?"

Allen and Michael looked concerned. Allen stood up from his chair. "Don't you remember what happened last night?"

Thinking back I tried to remember. Everything in my mind was a blur; I could only make out bits of it. "I remember that Michael and Anthony were over, we were having some kind of movie night, then I remember running down a hall and then it's dark."

Both of them looked at each other without saying anything. Allen sat back down. "It's not important. What's important is that you're awake now. I've already contacted your parents to let them know everything's fine and that I would keep them updated. Alessia said she'll be here shortly. Hopefully, we can get you out of here soon and back home."

I thought of how nice all that was but I was still concerned about where Anthony was. "What about Anthony? Is he all right? Why isn't he here?"

Michael started to say something but Allen shot him a look and he stopped. "Never mind that right now, just rest and I'll go let the nurse know you're awake." With that Allen stood up and walked out of the room.

Once Allen was gone and I was sure he was out of earshot, I looked over at Michael. "You were about to say something about Anthony. Where is he? Is everything all right? What in the hell happened last night and why can't I remember?"

Michael sighed. "I'll tell you later. I promise now is not the time. You gave us all a scare, David. I'm just glad you're safe and okay." With that, I figured it was best to drop it, but in my mind I was furious. How could Anthony not be here? His boyfriend was in the hospital. I had no clue why he wasn't here by my side. But Allen was here and it made me feel good to know that even with everything going on he still cared enough to stick around, and then there was Michael, a guy I barely knew, and he wanted to make sure I was okay as well. I closed my eyes and went back to sleep.

I awoke to the sound of Alessia's voice. "Oh my god, David, honey, what happened?" she said with concern as she grabbed me and gave me the biggest, longest hug of my life.

"I'm not sure. Allen and Michael think it's best to discuss it later."

Alessia stood up and went into full-on mum mode. "Oh, they do now, do they? Well, we'll just see about that. First off, who's Michael?" She turned to Michael. "Well, that must be you, and while I don't know you, if you have anything to do with why my sweet David is in the hospital bed, I will end you."

Michael looked at her and then at me. I just shrugged; there was no stopping Alessia when she went into protection mode. At that point, Allen walked back in, and Alessia's lasers set on him. "YOU."

Allen looked confused. "Me? What did I do?"

Alessia went on. "I don't know yet, but I know you played into this mess somehow, and when I find out, both you and Anthony are in for a world of hurt."

Just then Mark walked in. "Calm down, Alessia, I'm sure there's a perfect explanation for all of this, but now is not the place or time. Right now we need to focus on David."

Alessia came out from her rage and sat on the bed next to me. "I know, I just care for him so much and every time we turn around it seems Allen and Anthony are causing him pain."

Allen shot her an angry expression. "This is in no way my fault. David came to my door last night and when I asked why he was there he passed out, so I brought him here. I don't know what the hell was going on in his apartment, but when I went down there this one pointing over at Michael, and Anthony were in the middle of a fight." The room went deadly quiet after that as no one knew what to say.

I kept looking around at everyone: Allen sitting back in the chair, steaming, with his leg twitching like he wanted to be anywhere else but here, Mark in the doorway looking down the hall like he was waiting for something, Alessia still on the bed next to me cuddling me like a mother, and Michael sitting next to the bed, whose knuckles, I was only now just noticing, were pretty beat up like he'd been in a fight.

Just then the doctor walked in. "Ah, Mr. Ricci, good to see you're awake. Can we get some privacy so I can talk to him about his medical diagnosis, please?" He looked around at everyone but none of them were budging.

I looked at the doctor. "It's okay, they can all stay. This is my family and we all look out for each other."

The doctor looked around. "Okay, it's your call. Well, David, you passed out from what I can gather was a very serious panic attack. Have you been under a lot of stress lately? Have there been changes in your life that have been making it difficult to cope?"

I looked around the room at everyone. They were all acting like they weren't interested in what the doctor was asking. "Umm, yeah, there's been some stress, but I've dealt with anxiety and stress for years and never had an episode like this before."

The doctor patted my leg. "Well, I recommend going and seeing a counselor about this, and maybe even taking medications to help you better handle your anxiety and stress. I'll get this all written up and some referrals and we'll get you out of here soon, I promise." With that, he turned and walked from the room.

The room was so quiet you could hear a pin drop. Just then Allen stood from his chair and stormed off. Mark went chasing after him. I couldn't make out what they were saying but I could tell Mark was trying to get Allen to pull it together. Whatever was being said between the two of them, it was a very serious conversation. A few minutes later they came back into the room.

Allen sat back down and Mark called for Alessia so they could give us some space. Michael took the hint and excused himself to go find some drinks for everyone. The three of them left the room and left me and Allen sitting there in complete silence, not even looking at one another.

We sat there for what felt like forever before Allen finally broke the silence. "So how are you feeling?"

I looked at him. "I'm fine. Look, last night I shouldn't—"

He stopped me from finishing my sentence. "I read your letter, the one you slid under my door, and you're right. I don't want us to stop talking, but come on, David, you expected me to just be okay with you choosing Anthony over me? And now there's Michael, who I found literally beating the crap out of Anthony in the middle of your apartment telling him you should be with him."

I stared at him and for a moment I wanted to scream, but I didn't. "You're right. I'm sorry. I didn't fully think it through when I decided that I owed it to Anthony to give us a chance, but the more I started to remember last night the more I saw that was a mistake. As for Michael, I had no clue he felt that way; we hardly knew each other. I suspected he was wanting to see if there was any chemistry there but I didn't think it was that serious."

Allen put his hand on his chin and started to laugh a little. "Of course, you didn't see it. You're probably the worst person in the world at picking up on people's intentions."

We both started laughing, and it felt nice to have this moment with Allen even if he was still pissed at me; at least we were getting things out into the open somewhat.

Allen continued, "This is all my fault. Had I not been so mad at you and just understood that you didn't see what I was seeing, you would've never gotten so worked up and ended up here, and now they think you're mentally unwell and want you to go see a crazy doctor." Allen's voice was breaking and I could hear the sadness in his voice.

"Allen, no, this is no way your fault, you are not to blame for any of this, I've been putting these feelings of dread and fear off for such a long time that they finally won."

Allen now had a tear running down his cheek. "Had I just seen the signs better we could have addressed this together."

I got out of my bed and hugged him. "There's nothing you could have done differently. What's important is that you showed me you do truly care about our friendship and are a true friend by taking control and making sure I was taken care of. You could have slammed the door in my face and left me lying there in the hall but you didn't and for that, I will be forever grateful."

Allen was now full-on ugly crying into my shoulder. Just then we heard Alessia coming down the hall. Allen composed himself and I got back into the bed.

I was barely back in before Alessia was in the room, being the ray of sunshine she could be. "So my loves, are we all forgiven and friends again or do I need to start beating some sense into the two of you?"

The three of us laughed.

"We're fine. Allen will just have to live with the fact that he's a twit and I'm gormless."

Alessia looked at me in confusion. "Well, I'm just pretending I didn't hear you call him names in the same sentence as saying you two are better."

Just then Michael and Mark walked back into the room. "Any word on getting out of this depressing place, buddy?" Mark said with a smile on his face.

I just shook my head, no, and the four of them sat around the bed chatting, waiting for them to come to discharge me.

Finally, the nurse came in with all the paperwork I needed to be discharged. Everyone excused themselves so that I could get all the information I needed as well as get dressed. Thankfully Allen and Michael made sure to bring me some clothes so I didn't have to walk out of here looking like a total bum in PJs in the middle of the day. Once dressed, I headed out to the hall where everyone was waiting for me. All of us made sure we had everything and then we headed down the long hall to leave.

Once home, Alessia, Mark, and Allen all said their goodbyes and headed off to their respective places. Michael was getting ready to leave but I stopped him. "Hey, umm... We need to talk. Will you come in, please?"

Michael looked at me in a panic before agreeing to come in and talk. We went inside, I made us both some tea, and we sat down on the couch.

"So I want to know what happened last night after I ran out of here. Allen told me what he saw when he came down here and I want to hear it from you."

Michael looked like he was about to jump out of his skin. I just sat there waiting for him to respond, looking at him in what I hoped was an intense way. "Well, after you left, Anthony kept screaming. I was going to chase after you as it seemed he wasn't going to, but we ended up on the ground in a fight before I could."

I wasn't sure what to think of this. "So who started the fight?"

He looked at me straight in the eye. "I...guess...I did," he said, dragging out the last word. He then continued, "When I went to come after you, Anthony got in front of me and I pushed him out of my way. The next thing I knew we were wrestling each other to the ground and punches were being swung."

I just sat there processing this. "Well, I just have one more question. Allen mentioned to me that he overheard you telling Anthony that I should be with you over him?"

Michael's face turned bright red. He started to stammer over his words trying to explain himself, but I stopped him and went on, "Look, I'm flattered, and you're a sweet guy, but as you can tell my life is a complete cluster fuck. Not that I might not be interested down the road, but I think we should just be very good friends. What do you say?"

The look on his face went from fear to relief. "Oh my god, David, I felt like I was going to have a heart attack. I'm sorry that you had to find out that way, but you know what? You're right; we haven't known each other that long and our first true hangout ended in disaster." He laughed, trying to make light of it.

We chatted a little longer before he got up to leave. At the door when we were saying our goodbyes, I decided to make sure he knew how I felt. "Hey, I want to thank you for everything. You're a true friend."

He smiled, we hugged each other goodbye, and he walked down the hall to the elevator. I shut my door, and my phone buzzed. I looked down to see it was Anthony.

Chapter 27
I NEEDED YOU

I sat there looking at the notification on my phone, wondering if I should read his text or not. What was he going to say? Was this going to be the end of our relationship? *Should* this be the end of our relationship? What was his reasoning for not being at the hospital? I had so many questions, but at the same time, I was still so angry and confused about everything that happened last night. I finally opened it.

Hey babe, I hope you're okay. I am so, so sorry I wasn't there today but I had to take care of some things after everything that went down last night. I went to the hospital but they told me you were discharged so I'm heading to your place now. See you soon. Love you.

I was so mad that he didn't tell me why he wasn't there but it was sweet that he did show up even if it was late. I was so confused and was not looking forward to the fight that was going to come. How was he going to handle the whole thing with Michael, or that I ran out of the apartment and went to Allen's? This was going to be one of the hardest things I'd had to do and my anxiety was starting to rise by the second.

About an hour later there was a knock on my door. My heart was now racing, and I stood up and headed for the door. I opened it slowly, and there was Anthony, his face swollen and his left eye black and bruised. Michael had really done a number on his face. I felt so bad for him, but I was also still pissed that this was all his fault. I welcomed him in and we headed over to the couch to have what I expected to be a very uncomfortable conversation.

We sat down and made small talk, neither one of us wanting to address the elephant in the room. I don't know what possessed me, but I took my hand and placed it on his face next to his swollen eye. "Does it hurt? Are you okay? Is this why you weren't at the hospital today when I woke up?"

He knocked my hand away as he winced. I felt bad that it hurt, and touching it did not help at all.

"I'm fine. You should see Michael."

I laughed in my head as I had seen Michael and all he had was a couple of bruised knuckles. He would have known that had he been there for me. I was confused. Why was he being so kind and sweet? This was not normal for Anthony and I was getting sick to my stomach with the fear of waiting for the big fight. Why was he not addressing the issue, did he want me to be the one to bring it up? My head was spinning with all of this and I just wanted to get it over with. I decided that it would be best to rip the Band-Aid off instead of waiting for him to do it. "So about last night... I think we need to talk about what happened."

The look on his face changed from calm and collected to stressed and fearful. "I don't think there's anything to talk about," Anthony said quickly. "We tried to see if we could be friends with Michael and it didn't work out, so now we know that and can keep working on us."

I was so aggravated by the fact he was trying to blow this off, and had things played out differently maybe we could have blown it off, but the reality was I'd passed out from the stress. Michael was there for me and Anthony wasn't and I wanted to know why. "Where were you today? You should have been there for me when I was in hospital." I made sure I said this in a tone that showed him my frustration and disappointment.

He looked at me and frowned. "I know I wasn't there and I am so sorry, but I told you I had business to take care of and that I came by later but you were home already."

My frustration was now becoming anger, and I finally snapped. "WHAT COULD POSSIBLY HAVE BEEN MORE IMPORTANT THAN ME? FOR REAL, ANTHONY, I PASSED OUT IN THE MIDDLE OF A HALLWAY, AND IT'S YOUR FAULT."

His look of shock made me smile a little inside. "How can you blame me for this, David, I'm not to blame for your anxiety issues, you had those before we started dating and before last night." His defensiveness was making me even angrier. I couldn't believe that he was trying to act as if his constant putting me down and his cheating were not to blame for my issues. While they weren't the only factors, they'd made them worse.

We both sat there in silence for the next fifteen minutes, neither one of us looking at the other, before I finally asked, "So what does this mean for us and our relationship?"

Anthony looked up. "What do you mean? There's nothing wrong with our relationship. We're fine."

I could not believe he was still acting like he didn't just belittle me and put me down last night. I decided now was as good a time as ever to mention Michael was there for me at the hospital and I planned to continue to have a friendship with him. "Well, I wasn't sure as you weren't there for me today when everyone else was."

He looked at me with a confused face. "What do you mean? Who was everyone? Alessia and Mark?" he said in a tone that was almost mocking.

"Well, yes, Alessia and Mark, but also Allen and even Michael were there for me."

At the look of rage that came over his face at the mention of Allen and Michael, I thought to myself, *Oh shit, here comes the fight now.*

Minutes passed without a sound, just like the night before when the apartment building seemed oddly quiet. Anthony was just sitting there with a black stare on his face, but I could see the wheels turning in his head and that he was in deep thought. I didn't dare speak; I figured it was best to wait till he had completely gathered his thoughts.

Finally, he spoke. "I'm sorry I wasn't there. I should have been, you're right, but I'm having trouble with the fact that Michael was there. Why was he there?"

My stomach was in full-on backflip mode, but I was also still mad at him. I don't know what possessed me but I told him, "Well, he actually cared enough about me to be there for me in my time of need."

The look of anger and despair on his face told me everything. He was mad that I called him out, but also mad at himself for allowing me to feel that way. All of these mixed feelings were making it even harder to know that our relationship was probably going to end.

The more I sat there, the more upset I was getting. I decided I had to be the one to do it even though I really didn't want to, but I was starting to get overwhelmed and wanted this to end. I grabbed his hand and looked him in the eye. "I think it will be best for the both of us if maybe we take a break."

Anthony's eyes started to tear up. This was not the reaction I was expecting from him, and it honestly hurt me to see him so upset, but I could not shake the feeling of being mad that he caused this and then wasn't there when I needed him.

He was holding my hand tighter now, trying his hardest not to break down. "Please, David, don't do this. I know we've had our problems and last night was a disaster, but we can still make this work."

My heart sank listening to his plea, but I could not continue with this; we both needed space and maybe later we could try again. "I'm sorry, Anthony, I care for you, but both of us are not in a good place right now and I think we should take a break, work on ourselves, and then give this another try. What do you think?"

Anthony didn't say a word, he just shook his head in agreement, pulled me in, and gave me a tight hug while he softly wept into my shoulder. After a few minutes we released one another, and he stood up and walked out of the apartment.

I sat back down on the couch. My mind was spinning. I wasn't sure how to feel about everything or the fact that I had actually broken up with him and he didn't freak out on me. But now I was replaying the conversation back in my head and realized I'd done the same thing with him that I'd done with Allen: I made a promise that I didn't think I'd be able to keep. Why did I keep doing that? Was I trying to ruin my life, was this what self-sabotage looked like? I was getting hungry, so I stood up to make something to eat, but as I entered the kitchen, everything went dark.

Chapter 28
WHAT IS HAPPENING?

I awoke a few hours later lying face-first on the floor of my kitchen. I got myself off the ground as quickly as I could and was in a panic. Why had I passed out again? I hadn't gotten any of the warning signs like the night before. I was honestly scared, and the thought that I could just pass out at any moment without notice scared me even more. I didn't want to be alone now but who could I go to? I decided Alessia would be the best for this, so I texted her that I had passed out again and just woken up on the kitchen floor, and if she could please come over. Not even five minutes later there was a loud banging on my door.

I answered it to see Alessia. She quickly grabbed me and hugged me before literally dragging me to the couch. Mark and Allen followed through the door behind her. Once on the couch, she went into her full mama bear mode again. "So what happened? What made you pass out this time? What were you trying to do when it happened? Were there any warning signs?"

I was amazed she said all that without even stopping for breath. I smiled at her. "I was feeling hungry so I was heading to the kitchen to eat, and once I entered everything went black. I didn't even know I passed out till I regained consciousness and texted you."

Alessia stood. "I'm going to make you something to eat. Mark, come help me. Allen, you sit with David and see what else he remembers before he passed out."

Both Mark and Allen complied. Alessia loved it when people did what she said. She and Mark headed off into the kitchen, and Allen sat in the chair next to the couch.

He stared at me intently. I could feel his eyes peering into my soul as he looked at me. "Sooo, do you wanna tell me what happened? I don't think you just passed out from not eating."

I looked down at the floor in the hopes that this was all a dream, but when I looked back up he was still there staring me down. "It's nothing, we don't have to talk about it. Really, I don't want to make you any more uncomfortable than you already are, having to be around me when I know you would rather be anywhere else."

He frowned at my words. "Jeez, David, I swear, your lack of understanding and being able to read the room is mind-blowing."

He was about to continue, but just then Mark walked into the room. "So, has he told you what happened yet?"

Allen stood from his chair. "No, maybe you'll have better luck. I can't deal with him right now." With that, he walked off into the kitchen.

Mark looked at me with confusion as he sat down in the chair. "What was that all about?" I just looked at him and shrugged. Mark leaned forward. "Look, David, I know you think you're being a burden, but you're not. Alessia cares deeply about you, as do I, and if the shoe was on the other foot you would be there for us, so tell me what's up."

I frowned, then put my head between my legs. "I don't know, Mark, everything has just been shit lately. First I fucked up everything with Allen and he can't stand to be around me, then everything with Anthony and Michael. I just can't seem to do anything right and no one can be this dumb."

Mark just stared at me, not saying a word. We just sat there, waiting for one of us to break the silence, and just then Allen returned. Once Allen was back in the room Mark turned his attention to him. "You, me, kitchen. NOW," he said in an angry tone. I was startled by this, but Mark got up from the chair and dragged Allen back into the kitchen.

I could hear them arguing but couldn't make out what was being said. I strained to hear but wasn't getting enough to piece together what they were saying or what Mark was so mad about. I knew I was the topic, but why was Mark so mad? Just then Allen came into the room and rushed past the couch and out the door of the apartment. I was so confused and wondered if I should go after him to make sure he was okay. I stood up but just then Alessia came into the room with the food she had made, so I sat back down on the couch.

I ate while the three of us made small talk, but the whole time I was wondering what had happened between Allen and Mark. Was I going to be the cause of their friendship ending? Why was Allen so mad and why had he rushed out of the apartment like that? After a few more minutes of my mind not settling, I had to know. "Soooo... Are we going to talk about Allen just rushing out of here?"

Mark and Alessia just looked at one another, then Alessia grabbed my hand. "It's not important, he'll be back, just a little disagreement among friends. Besides, we're more worried about you and what caused you to pass out. Tell us what you were doing before you went into the kitchen."

I frowned. This wasn't going to end until I told them, was it? Well, I guess I did call them over so I might as well tell them. "I was sitting here on the couch, having mixed feelings and trying to get them under control after Anthony had left."

They both looked concerned but Alessia was the one to speak up. "Anthony was over? What happened, hun?"

I took a drink of the tea that was sitting in front of me. "Well, it was really weird. He came over acting as if everything was fine, which I was concerned about as his face was all torn up from last night, then we had a long talk, and I...kinda...broke up with him, but also kinda accidentally promised him that we might be able to make it work later."

The look of shock on both of their faces said it all. They didn't even have to say anything and I could tell what they were both thinking. Alessia just hugged me. Mark was playing with his phone trying to act as if he hadn't heard what I just said.

Alessia let go and said, "Are you okay? How did he handle it? Was there a fight, is that what caused you to pass out?"

I just smiled. "No, there wasn't a fight. He took it pretty hard and cried and I felt bad for him, but I couldn't get over the fact that he wasn't there for me today. Apparently, he had business to take care of."

Mark looked up from his phone for a second then went right back to what he was doing. Alessia and I chatted some more, and after a little while, the two of them headed back to her apartment and I went and took a shower.

After I was out of the shower and getting dressed, there was a knock on my door. I finished getting my clothes on and went to answer it. When I opened the door there was no one there, just a box with a note. I picked it up and sat it down on the table. I took the note and opened it.

Dear David, in this box, is why I wasn't at the hospital today. I hope this will make you understand. Love Anthony.

I put the note aside and turned my attention to the box. It was nothing special, just a plain brown box. I was wondering what was in it that could be considered more important than me. I opened the box and started to remove the packing paper.

Once all the paper was removed, I peered inside, and to my surprise, a stuffed bear was wearing a t-shirt with the Scottish flag on it, a picture from mine and Anthony's time in Scotland, and lastly, a second note.

David, our time in your village made me realize you are the one for me. I'm sorry for everything I've put us through and know that we are better together. I'm ready to start being friends with Allen again as that will make you happy and us better as a couple.

Forever yours, Anthony.

I felt like such an ass. I wanted to call him, but I also was still confused as to why he didn't just tell me this or bring the stuff with him earlier when he came over. I decided I had to go find him, so I grabbed a jumper and headed for the door.

Just as I opened the door, I screamed. Allen was standing there. The sound of the scream made him jump back. "What the hell, Allen, you scared me."

Allen laughed. "What do you mean I scared you? You're the one opening doors screaming."

We both laughed. "Hey look, I'm sorry but I'm just heading out. Can this wait?"

I started to pass him and head down the hall, but before I could make it to the elevator, Allen said as clearly as he could, "I'm in love with you, David."

I stopped dead in my tracks and turned around slowly. "What did you just say?" I asked to make sure I'd heard him correctly and not just what I wanted to hear.

Allen was still standing in front of my door. "You heard me. I said I'm in love with you."

I smiled. "Well, you have a funny way of showing it, you know." The door to the elevator opened and I walked in.

Just as the door was closing, Allen's foot came in, blocking it. "What do you think you're doing? You can't just walk away from me like that."

I just stared at him in confusion before I leaned into him. "I can't just walk away? You're the one who ran out earlier, now you're telling me I can't walk away from this conversation? You don't get to tell me what I can and cannot do, understand?"

With that, he removed his foot from the door and it closed. While waiting for the elevator to get to the main floor, I was wondering if I'd just made the biggest mistake of my life, and would this really be the nail in the coffin of Allen and I ever having a romantic relationship? I was second-guessing myself, thinking maybe I should go back and try to fix it, but what about Anthony and his gift? I decided I needed to go see Anthony first; I could always try to mend my and Allen's relationship later.

The elevator reached the first floor and the doors opened. I started to exit, and as I was walking towards the door I felt someone grab my arm and spin me around. The next thing I knew there I was in the middle of the lobby locked in a kiss with Allen. I have to admit I enjoyed Allen's kisses, but I also felt this dance was getting old. I pulled myself away from him. "What the fuck, Allen?"

He just frowned. "I was hoping it would remind you how much we care for one another."

I smiled and started to laugh; he was right, I cared so deeply for him that it almost hurt. I hugged him, told him I had to go take care of some business, and went on my way.

I walked out into the street more confused than ever. The day was cold and the streets were crowded with everyone returning to school from their holiday. Soon classes would start back up again and everyone was scrambling to prepare. I made my way toward Anthony's apartment, and on my way, I passed the restaurant where Michael worked. Thankfully I was able to make it past unnoticed. I didn't even know if he was there, but I seemed to have the bad luck of running into him everywhere so I was glad that I didn't this time. I made it to Anthony's apartment building and walked into the lobby. I entered the elevator and went up to his floor, and once there I went right to his door to knock, but before I did I could hear him talking, so I listened for a bit.

He was on the phone with someone, telling them about mine and his conversation, and how I broke his heart, but how he'd still left the gifts that he had made for me at my door. I felt that I needed to knock so he knew I was there, but just as I lifted my hand I heard some more of Anthony's conversation. "Thanks, Trevor, I can't wait to see you this weekend." My heart hurt. I lowered my hand. He was talking to Trevor about us. The same Trevor that he cheated on me with? I felt sick and stupid for coming. I turned quickly and headed back out of his building before he could have any idea I was there.

I was rushing back to my apartment, just wanting to hide from the world. These last few days had been a complete mess and it was all my fault. I was hurrying so fast that I was not paying attention to the world around me. I was bumping into people, slipping on icy spots on the walk, and of course, with the luck I was having, I even managed to run straight into Michael. I hit him so hard that we both fell to the ground. I looked down to see him lying flat on his back.

"Well, hello, David, nice to see you."

We both started laughing. "Oh my god, Michael, are you all right?" I asked as I was picking myself up from on top of him and then helping him to his feet.

"Well, I always wanted you to push me down but not in this manner."

Again we both laughed.

"Are you all right, why are you rushing so fast?" he asked with a note of concern as he placed his hand on my shoulder.

I smiled. "Yeah, I'm all right, just trying to get home."

Michael, still with his hand on my shoulder, said, "You're not feeling like you're going to pass out again, are you?"

I sat there frozen, not wanting to answer him. I hadn't even thought about passing out again but his mentioning it made me sick to my stomach even more than I already was. "No, no, I don't feel like that, I'm just really cold."

With that he smiled, kissed me on the cheek, and walked off. Jeez, why did he kiss my cheek, why was it that all of a sudden this pale-faced, red-headed, heavy-accented guy who'd never had any luck with relationships now had three guys who were all interested in him? Was I some kind of prize in America, being from another country? I could not get my mind to settle the whole rest of the walk home.

Once I was back in my apartment feeling safe and sound, I changed into some comfortable clothes, made myself something to eat with a hot cup of tea, sat down on the couch, and watched some horrible documentary on girlfriends who killed their boyfriends. It was not the best thing to watch in my state of mind, but I just found it so interesting. I finally headed off to bed to try and forget this whole ordeal from the past two days.

Chapter 29
REALIZATIONS

A month had passed since all of the unpleasantness with everyone had gone on. I had not heard from or seen Anthony in that time and while there were days I missed him, I was also still very pissed off at him. My interactions with Michael were also to a minimum. I found it best to keep my distance as I was afraid he would not truly give me the space I needed to figure all of this out. As for Allen, we would talk with one another in passing, but each time I could feel the tension and it was always so awkward so we tried to keep it short each time for both our sanities. Alessia and I were making it a point to make sure we spent time together weekly. I would text Sam daily so she knew I was okay. Ever since that day I passed out she and my parents had been trying to get me to come home, so I compromised and said I would give Sam daily updates. I was enjoying my classes, had started some therapy, there were no more fainting episodes, and things were going as well as I could have hoped.

With my therapy, I learned to start to love and respect myself more. I was no longer in this constant feeling of dread, and I enjoyed waking up and getting out more than I ever had. I also liked my therapist. He was calming and not judgmental, allowed me to control our time together, and helped me better understand what it was that I wanted in life. The one thing I dreaded the most was that starting today when I saw him, he wanted to start looking into how I'd handled my and Anthony's relationship, and I was not looking forward to it. But I think he was right that they needed to be addressed if I was to ever move on and have a healthy relationship in my life, not just romantically but also with friends and family.

My last class just finished for the day and I was to head right over to see him. Thankfully it was a short walk, and the weather, while still cold at the end of February, was nice. I was walking to his office watching as everyone moved in all directions, trying not to be late for their next class, when I caught something out of the corner of my eye. I looked to see what caught my attention, and standing there across the diag was Anthony. He was locked in a kiss with some girl I had never seen on campus before. I guessed he was still not comfortable kissing guys in public and was over us, it seemed. I felt sick to my stomach, so I shook it off and continued to my session.

Once there I checked in and waited to be called. Only a few minutes had passed before the door to his office opened. "Ah, David, right on time as always. Please come in."

I grabbed my bag and headed into his office, which was much larger on the inside than it looked from the lobby. There was a wall of windows, a couch, two chairs, plus his desk. He never sat at the desk, he would always sit in one of the chairs, and I usually took the other. We both sat down.

"So how are you feeling today? Anything you want to get off your chest or should we dive into your relationships?"

I frowned. "Well, actually, what I want to talk about is on my way here I saw Anthony, and he was...kissing some girl in the middle of campus."

The therapist just sat there; he did this a lot when he wanted me to continue so he could gather more information.

"It made me feel sick. I was upset because it seems he's moved on from us, but also because he would never kiss me in public."

He leaned back in his chair. "I see. So to me, it sounds like it's not so much him moving on, it's the fact that he always hid your relationship, except if I recall the time he came to your home where no one knew who he was."

I sat there for a moment and thought about what he just said. Could it be true? Was I not upset about him moving on but the fact that he hid me? The more I thought about it the more I realized he was right. I didn't care about Anthony and our relationship; the only reason I was with him was because I had low self-esteem and he showed an interest in me. I let my therapist know this and we worked on this for a little longer, figuring out how I could manage my feelings when I saw him in public with other people and how to remind myself that I was worth more.

We were about halfway into the session when he dropped the bomb I had been waiting for. "So what about you and Allen? Your obsession with him could be seen as unhealthy."

I felt like I wanted to crawl out of my skin. "I don't see it as unhealthy. I care deeply for Allen and it's clear he does for me as well. I've just fucked it all up with how I treated him and the whole Anthony situation."

He stared at me intently. "And how did Michael play into all that?"

I didn't know how to answer that so I just sat there looking down at the floor. He continued, "Could it be the reason you pushed Allen away and stayed with Anthony, then brought Michael into the mix, was because you were afraid of falling in love? Because if you did that, what would it mean for the life you have planned for yourself after school?"

I sat there for a second thinking about this before I spoke. "I don't have my life planned after school."

He again leaned back in his chair. "I think you do, deep down. You know that you'll go back home and help your grandparents with the farm and eventually take over because it's the safe thing to do, and also because you have fond memories of Allen there, and if you can't have him, because you're afraid to lose him or fall in love, this is the next best thing."

I sat there in shock. How could he know that? I had not mentioned to anyone that I wanted to go home, but he was right, it had crossed my mind to take over the farm many times over the past month.

For the rest of the session, we tied up some loose ends to issues we had touched on in the past and made a plan for what we would like to accomplish next time, and then he gave me homework to think about my life if I did go home, or if I didn't and allowed myself to be loved, either by Allen or someone else. This gave me a lot to think about and I headed home to get started. The last task he had was for me to also decide in what capacity, if any, I wanted Anthony in my life.

Once in my apartment, I sat down and thought about Anthony. I wanted him in my life, that much I knew, but I didn't think we could ever be more than friends, not after everything we went through and his inability to be proud enough to show me off to anyone as his boyfriend. I wrote him a letter explaining that I did want us to have a relationship on a close friend's level and that I'd seen him kissing the girl on campus so I was not wanting a romantic relationship with him.

As for thinking about my life if I didn't go home... What if I did stay? I could theoretically see myself with someone and being happy. It was what my parents wanted for me, but my mind kept coming back to Allen. I kept picturing us together, riding the horse around the farm, running through the streets of London, going to the musical, and watching him play his cello or violin. I hadn't heard him play since that night in his apartment, and I missed it. Then it dawned on me that what I wanted most in this life was Allen. It didn't matter if we were on the farm or here in the States; what would make me happy was allowing myself to be loved and to let him love me. I quickly stood up from my seat and ran for my door. I didn't know what I was going to do or say but I had to go and see Allen at this very moment.

I rushed down the hall to the stairs. I was in no mood to wait for the elevator. I ran up the stairs as fast as I could and down his hall. I was panting when I got to his door and knocked hard. He answered the door, seeing me there still trying to catch my breath. "David, are you all right? You're not about to pass out again, are you?"

I grabbed his face with both hands, pulled him in, and locked him in the deepest and most passionate kiss we'd ever had.

We pulled away for a few minutes, both of us trying to catch our breaths. "I am in love with you, Allen, we both know I have been for a long time. I finally feel worthy enough to take you up on your plea back in my parents' parlor to love and protect me."

The smile on Allen's face was the biggest I had ever seen. He pulled me in and kissed me again. "I love you, David, and I promise things will be better from now on."

We embraced each other for a little longer before I looked down at my feet and noticed I'd run out with no shoes. "Well, I should probably get back to my place, seeing as I seem to be missing shoes."

Allen looked down, and we both laughed, then we kissed goodbye. I told him I would call him later and headed back down to my apartment.

Once back in my apartment, I looked at the pile of mail that I had to take down. I grabbed the letter I had written to Anthony and walked back and forth with it in my hand, contemplating what I should do. Should I send it, or should I change it and tell him about me and Allen? I looked down at the letter in my hands. I thought about everything he had done, with Trevor and pretending we weren't a couple in public, causing the fight with Michael, moving on within a month of us breaking up, and I tore the letter up and threw it in the trash.

Chapter 30
WHAT A DAY

The next few weeks went by without any issues. Allen and I were doing great, not having to deal with Anthony and his drama had been doing wonders for my mental health, Alessia and I had been spending a lot of time together, and I felt bad for as she was ditching Mark to spend time with me. I would tell her it was okay to spend time with him as I worried that it would cause issues with their relationship, but they both assured me it wasn't; still, deep down, I felt bad.

Everything was looking up, but while these past few weeks had been great, I knew I was going to have to address the elephant in the room. My therapist would keep bringing it up every week that I needed to confront Anthony and Michael on what kind of relationships we were going to have. I was all for having some kind of friendship with Michael, and Allen and I had even had a discussion about it and he was okay with it if I wanted to be his friend, but as for Anthony, I didn't want to see him yet. I wasn't sure if I even could.

With all of the things going on I was trying my hardest to make sure I achieved high marks this term. With everything that had happened, I'd let my grades slip and had been working hard to get them back up. I'd been doing well lately, so I figured today after school I would invite Michael over and see what we could come up with. We had texted periodically over the last few weeks but hadn't hung out. I wasn't sure if he would even want to, but I figured it was worth a try. I wanted to have this done before the end of the term and it was coming up fast, so I was running out of time.

Once class was out for the day I pulled out my phone and texted Michael.

Hey, would you wanna come by tonight and hang out, just the two of us? I promise it won't end the same as last time :)

I put my phone away and headed for home. Once there, I put my bag down by the door, went into the kitchen, and made myself a cup of tea, then sat down on the couch. I checked my phone to see if Michael had responded. There was a text from him so I opened it.

Hey David, I would love to hang out, but I have to work tonight. How about tomorrow?

We texted back and forth for a bit and made plans to hang out tomorrow.

I sat there wondering what I should do with my evening. Mark and Alessia were out on a dinner date, Sam was busy with her studies, and Allen had to stay at school late tonight to work on his performance for his end-of-term project. I had no one I could hang out with and I was all caught up in my class work. I decided to read a book that Mum had gotten me that I had been putting off. I pulled it off the bookshelve and started flipping the pages. I was really in no mood to read it, so I threw it on the table before I decided I would go surprise Allen by bringing him some dinner to his practice hall.

I went into the kitchen, cooked some food for the two of us, and made sure to pack it up all nice before going out the door. I made my way down the crowded street towards Allen's class. It took some navigation to find his room, and once in front of the door I sat and waited for the music to stop. In typical Allen fashion, I could hear his emotions being poured into his performance. He had a theme to his songs; this time he was playing "Shallow." Allen must have a thing for *A Star is Born*, as this was the second time he had played a song from it. I waited till I heard the playing stop, then I knocked.

There was some shuffling inside before Allen opened the door. He looked at me with an expression of surprise, confusion, and happiness. "David, babe, what are you doing here?"

I smiled at him. "I thought I would surprise you with some dinner." I held up the food I'd made, and he smiled, let me into the room, and we sat down to eat. We chatted about our days, I complimented his beautiful playing as always, and joked with him that he was going to run out of songs if he didn't pick a different show to play from. We both laughed and were having a good time. I let him know about my plan to have Michael over the next day to see if we could have a friendship, which he had no issue with, and we made up a plan in case things didn't go well. Afterwards, we packed up. It was getting late so Allen packed his cello away and we walked home together.

Once back at our apartment building, Allen walked with me to my door, and then leaned in to kiss me goodbye. I, however, had other plans. Once we were kissing, I pulled him into my apartment and closed the door behind us. I pushed him up against the door as we kept making out. We were getting more heated by the second, our hands moving all over each other's bodies. I pulled away from Allen for a second and pulled off my shirt. Allen took the hint and his came off right after. He picked me up as we continued to make out and carried me over to the couch. There things heated up, and we had a long passionate time. This was the first time we had done this and it was perfect. It felt different than with Anthony, as this time it wasn't just meaningless sex but true passion.

After we were done, we put our underwear back on. Allen was wearing these sexy low-cut ones I had never seen before, and honestly, it was making it hard to avert my gaze. I headed into the kitchen and made some tea. When I returned, Allen was sitting there in the buff. I laughed. "Who do you think I am, Superman? I need a break before I can go a second round." He laughed, grabbed his cup of tea from my hand, and sat back down on the couch. I sat next to him, and we cuddled for a while before we drifted off to sleep in each other's arms.

I awoke before Allen the next morning. I slid myself from under his arm and headed off to the kitchen to make us some breakfast. I started to cook and make the tea, trying to be as quiet as I could so as not to wake him. I was almost done when I heard Allen behind me. "Well, good morning, handsome, what are we doing?"

I turned to see him standing there smiling. "Good to see you have at least some clothes on," I said with a laugh as I sat the food down on the table. Allen smiled, walked over to me, pulled his shirt off, then sat down at the table. I just smiled and sat down across from him, and we ate our breakfast and chatted about what was planned for the day. Allen was going to work more on his music for the end of term, and I was just going to get the apartment ready for later tonight when Michael came over and go do some shopping.

After we had finished eating, Allen helped me clean up the kitchen and do the dishes, and then we both took a shower together before we got dressed. Afterward, Allen and I kissed goodbye and he headed off to his apartment. Once I shut the door and locked it behind him, I sat myself on the couch and thought about last night and how great it was. Things were going well and after last night I would say *very* well. I smiled before getting started with my day.

Chapter 31
CAN WE BE FRIENDS?

After getting the apartment cleaned up to a level that would not make my mum cringe, I went out to get the shopping done. I made my way down the street to the local market as I just needed a few things for the dinner I was planning with Michael. Once at the shop, I grabbed a basket and started heading up and down the aisles to see if anything else caught my eye. I rounded the corner into the next aisle and ran into Anthony.

We both just stood there for a second, looking at one another. I finally decided that I would rather have an awkward conversation over this awkward silence. "Oh, Anthony, hey, it's good to see you. How have you been?"

He smiled. "Hey David, it's good to see you. How are you? I've been doing good, just been really working on myself in the hopes we can eventually get back on track."

Hearing him say this complete lie made me angry, but this was not the time or place to call him out on his bullshit. We had a quick chat before I excused myself to finish my shopping. Once finished, I headed for the till, paid for my items, and returned to my apartment.

I'd started to put the shopping away when I heard the text notification on my phone. I opened it and saw Anthony's name.

Hey, it was good to see you today. Can I swing by and chat about us?

I figured it was as good a time as any to have this conversation. It would come out sooner or later that Allen and I were together and that I saw him the other day on the diag. I texted him back saying it was okay but that I didn't have long.

A few minutes later there was knocking on my door. I answered and let Anthony in and we sat down on the couch. We both sat there and looked down at the floor before Anthony began. "So...have you had any time to think about us?"

I looked up from the floor. "Well, I saw you on the diag the other day kissing that lady... Sooo Allen and I kinda got together."

Anthony looked at me for a minute, trying to gather his thoughts. "Oh, you saw that, huh? Look, David, I'm sorry. I was just confused and I'm struggling with being in a same-sex relationship publicly. Everyone I've ever been with was okay with keeping it a secret. You understand, right?"

I just looked at him with a frown. "Well, that's not good enough for me, Anthony, and Allen is willing to be public about us. I care for you deeply and want you in my life, but I think we'll be better off as just friends. Do you think that can ever happen?"

Anthony stood. I assumed it was so he could start yelling, so I stood also in case I needed to get away, but instead he smiled at me. "You know what, I care for you too much to let us not be friends."

I smiled back at him. We hugged each other, and when we went to let go, Anthony stole a kiss. I pulled back, furious. "Seriously, Anthony."

He just smiled as we walked towards the door. "I'll see you later, stud." He winked as he walked out my door and shut it behind him.

I sat on the couch, replaying the conversation in my head to see if I'd given him any indication that it was okay to go for a kiss. I couldn't see anything that would have given him that idea. I was so mad that I wasn't sure we would be able to be friends if he was going to pull shit like that. What would have happened had Allen been over? He would have flipped out, which would have led to them fighting. I decided to put it out of my mind as I had to start getting ready for Michael to come over. I was just hoping that I would have better luck with him than I had with Anthony in being able to have an honest platonic friendship.

The day had turned into the evening, and Michael would be over soon. I went into the kitchen and started to cook dinner for the two of us. At the same time, Allen and I were texting back and forth, making sure that I was going to be okay. He reassured me he would be home soon if I needed him. I was finishing up when Michael texted me to let me know he was down in the lobby and would be up in a few minutes. I managed to get the food plated and set on the table just as there was a knock on the door.

I walked over and answered it. Michael was standing there smiling. "Hey David, it's so good to see you." He pulled me in for a hug.

"It's nice to see you too, Michael, please come in. I cooked us dinner. I hope you like it." With that, I led him inside and we sat down to eat. Everything was going great; we talked about that night with Anthony and had a good laugh, and about how things had been going for each of us. I even told him about Allen and me, and when I mentioned this Michael got this weird look on his face.

"Soo I guess this isn't a date then?"

I looked at him, confused. "Why would you think this was a date?" I asked, wondering what had given him that impression. We both sat there in silence for what felt like hours.

We both were eating our food quietly when Michael looked up. "I guess I thought that this might have been a date because you invited me over and then cooked this dinner."

I realized he had a point. I frowned while thinking how stupid I was to make dinner. I thought I was doing something nice for a friend but Michael had feelings for me. It was my fault for not making it clear what my intentions were at the start. I looked at him. "I'm so sorry, I didn't think anything of it. I was just trying to do something nice for a friend. That's why I invited you over, to see if we could be friends with me being with Allen. I want to be friends but I understand that it might be uncomfortable for you."

He was looking down, playing with his food. "I would love to be your friend, David, but we've been having issues in that department."

Again it went silent. The both of us finished eating with very few words. Once I cleaned up we headed out into the living room and sat down on the couch. I continued our conversation. "You're right, we've not been clear with our relationship up to this point and I want to change that."

Michael smiled. "Yeah, I think that's for the best."

I was feeling better about this now and felt that it would be fine to have this conversation. "So, what I was thinking is that we try being plain old platonic friends."

Michael laughed. "Plain old friends, huh? Well, that sounds boring. How about platonic friends who occasionally flirt with one another?"

We both laughed. It was nice that this was going so well. We came to the agreement that we could be friends and friends only and that he would respect the boundaries of Allen and me.

After that, we watched some movies. I texted Allen to let him know that it was going well and that Michael and I had agreed to just be friends, that he was going to respect our relationship and not interfere, and that maybe the three of us could even do dinner sometime. Allen thought this was all fine. We texted a little longer before he had to go to sleep. I turned my attention back to Michael. Neither of us was getting into the movie so we switched to video games. I had not played my game system in so long, but we had a blast. Michael was much better than I expected him to be, and we played for hours until it was well past midnight, when Michael looked at his watch. "Oh wow, look at the time. It's one a.m. How did we let time slip away from us? I should go, you must want to sleep."

I looked at him in confusion. I was having fun, why would I want it to end? Plus it was so late, and I didn't want him to have to walk home; it wouldn't be safe. "Don't be crazy, you're staying here tonight. I won't let you walk home at this hour."

We went back and forth about him leaving before he finally caved in and agreed to stay.

We finished up our game and I went into my room to get ready for bed. While changing, there was a knock on my bedroom door, and once I had my pants on I answered to see what Michael needed. "Is everything all right?"

Michael smiled. "Yeah, I'm fine, I was just wondering if I could take a shower?"

I smiled, showed him to the bathroom in my room, and let him know I would be back with a clean towel. When I came back I heard the water running so I figured it was safe to enter. When I opened the door, Michael had not gotten in the shower yet, but he had undressed. It took everything I had to look down. Michael laughed, hopping behind the curtain, and I excused myself.

I went and sat on my bed. A few minutes later Michael appeared at the door in the towel, and I looked at him. "Oh, hey, I'm sorry I walked in on you. When I heard the water I thought you were in the shower already."

He laughed. "It's okay, we're friends so I didn't mind." With that, he went back into the bathroom before returning shortly in his boxers and shirt. We said goodnight before he headed out to the living room to sleep on the couch.

I lay there in my bed looking up at the ceiling. Aside from walking in on him naked, things had gone well today. He didn't try to get me to join him, he didn't try to sleep in my bed, and he was understanding of mine and Allen's relationship. It was nice to know that I was able to make one friend out of this mess. Still, I thought about Anthony and what had happened. Why was he not getting the hint? I kept running the whole day over and over in my head before I drifted off to sleep.

The next morning I turned over in my bed and in a second I realized there was someone next to me. I jumped out and screamed. Well, this scared him as much as it scared me as in a second I heard Michael's voice. "David, what's wrong?" He was now standing on the other side of my bed.

I just stared at him, my heart racing, before I yelled, "What do you mean what's wrong? Why are you in my bed?"

A look of confusion came over his face, then he laughed. "You don't remember? Last night I came in and asked if I could sleep on the other side of the bed as it was freezing in your living room and you said yes. We shared the bed, that's it. Nothing else happened, I promise."

I sat there for a second trying to remember. I leaned against the door to the bathroom and then started laughing loudly. "Oh, I thought that was a dream. I forgot you were here." We both started laughing at one another. After a few minutes of laughing and waiting for our hearts to stop racing, Michael grabbed his pants, put them on, and went into the kitchen to make us some tea while I got dressed.

Once dressed I headed into the main room to find Michael had made tea for both of us and had even started making breakfast. As I walked into the kitchen Michael said, "I hope you don't mind, I figured since you cooked last night, I'd cook this morning. It's the least I can do after almost giving you a heart attack."

I smiled and sat down at the table and started drinking my tea while he finished the cooking. Once he was done, Michael put down nice-looking plates of eggs and bacon with toast. We ate and laughed about scaring one another and then talked about life and our plans for after term. I still hadn't decided if I was going home or staying here for the summer. Michael was planning to do some world traveling, which sounded exciting.

After we finished eating, I cleaned up the kitchen. Michael tried to help but he wasn't very good at cleaning the dishes. Once I had finished getting things put away, Michael managed to get dressed, we said our goodbyes, and he headed out the door. I went and took a shower, and while in there I ran in my mind over and over how the evening and this morning had gone, and it was nice. I think Michael and I could be great friends; he just needed to stay out of my bed in the future.

Chapter 32
THE CHOICE IS YOURS

The next few weeks were quiet. Allen and I had not seen much of each other, both being busy with our studies and getting ready for finals. Michael and I texted a few times but had not seen each other since that day I woke up to find him in my bed. Alessia made it a point to see me daily as Mark was busy and she was bored out of her mind. Everything was going well till Allen texted me that he wanted to talk.

I kept stressing myself out overthinking what he could want to talk about. Was he over us already and wanted to end things? Was Anthony right and this was some long con of a joke Allen was playing? I knew these weren't true, but I couldn't keep them from filling my mind and making me sick to my stomach with worry.

Mum and Dad wanted me to call them so we set up a video chat on the computer so that we could all see each other and I figured it would be easier than trying to talk to both of them at the same time. I sat down on the couch, opened my laptop, and called them. Mum answered in seconds. "David, sweetie, it's so good to see you. How are you, honey?"

It was nice to see Mum smile and hear her voice. We didn't talk as much as either of us would have liked, but we always made the best of it when we did.

"Hi Mum, is Dad there with you? I thought you both wanted to talk?"

She smiled. "He'll be here in a minute. So tell me, how's Allen?"

I thought it was sweet that she asked about him. "He's good, though we haven't seen much of each other with the term coming to an end."

We made more small talk while we waited for Dad to arrive home.

While Mum and I were talking I could hear Dad come in the door. Mum looked up from the computer. "Oh good, you're home. David is on so we can have our chat."

Dad said something but I didn't hear what he said, and a few seconds later his face appeared on the screen next to Mum's. "Ahh, David, I was starting to think you had forgotten about your mum and dad." He smiled and laughed.

I smiled and rolled my eyes. "Like I could ever forget you two," I said in a joking manner.

Dad made small talk while Mum went to get them both some tea. We talked about school and how classes were going, how Dad had been doing with work, and some of the things he had been doing lately.

Once Mum returned and sat the cups down, the looks on their faces went from cheerful to more serious. Mum looked into the camera. "So, I know we've been pushy on this a few times but your dad and I really want to know what your plans are for the summer. Will you be coming home or are you staying in the States?"

I sat there for a moment. I hadn't spent any time thinking about it and still wasn't sure what I wanted to do. I frowned. Dad must have picked up on this as he said, "Hey look, kiddo, you can do whatever you want, we're not trying to force you, we just want to know if we're planning a holiday for three or two. If you want to stay there or travel with friends, we understand. Your mum and I will go on holiday and see you after, or you can come home for half the time. It's completely up to you, so don't stress about it." Once he finished there was an awkward pause and silence fell over the room.

After some time had passed, I finally responded. "I'm not sure yet. I would love to see you and a holiday for the three of us sounds like fun."

I paused again, and Mum chimed in. "Well, we don't need your answer now, we just wanted to make sure you had time to think about it. Just let us know by the end of the term."

With that, we changed the subject. Mum filled me in on Grandma and Grandad, and we talked more about what they were planning for a holiday before we ended the call. I then cleaned up the living room so I could get ready for Allen to come over to talk about whatever it was he had on his mind.

I was starting to get overwhelmed waiting for Allen to show up. The more time passed the more my stomach was once again trying to win an Olympic gold medal. I had to try and settle this. I texted Sam, hoping she would be able to respond in time.

Hey, spoke with Mum and Dad today, they were wondering what I was planning for the summer holiday. Now Allen is on his way over...he said he has something we need to talk about. I am losing my mind over what it could be.

Thankfully before I could even put my phone down there was a reply from Sam.

Well, what is your summer plan? As for Allen, I'm sure it's nothing. He probably just wants to see you since you two have been busy.

I calmed a bit on the Allen topic as she was probably right, but now Sam was asking what my plans for the summer were. Why did everyone care so much? Was there a reason they wanted me to come back to Scotland? Was I missing something? We texted a little longer about what Mum, Dad, and I had discussed, and what her plans were. She didn't know what she was doing either, and when I heard a knock at the door we said our goodbyes so I could go let Allen in.

I opened the door to see Allen smiling but what was more of a surprise was that he had a gift bag with him. I tried to look inside but he pulled it away. "Well, aren't we being a bit of an eager beaver."

We laughed as he came inside and headed over to the couch. Once we were both settled, I wanted to get this dreaded feeling I had out of the way. "So what was it that you wanted to talk about?" I asked quickly without trying to show that my anxiety was rising by the second.

Allen just smiled, grabbed the bag, and sat it in my lap. I looked at him for a second, confused. He didn't say anything, just sat there smiling. I opened the bag and started to pull out the items inside.

The more I dug in the bag the more confused I became. There was a hiking backpack, a bottle of wine, a little Napoleon figure, and a little Eiffel Tower. I looked up at him.

"Keep going, there's more," he said with an excited tone in his voice like he was a kid on Christmas.

I dug down into the bag once more and pulled out an envelope. There was nothing written on it, and Allen was not giving any hints as to what was inside, so I opened it. When I pulled out the piece of paper and opened it, I could not believe my eyes. Inside were two tickets to France. I looked back at him. He still had a big smile and there was a twinkle in his eye that made me feel calm all of a sudden. I just sat there, stunned.

After what felt like an hour but was surely more like a few minutes, Allen finally said, "Well?"

I just looked at him. "Well, what?"

Allen's smile turned into a frown. "What do you mean what? I bought us tickets to France so we can go hiking in the southern part together this summer."

I just sat there looking at the tickets in my hand. "I don't know what to say, Allen, this is an amazing gift, but what about spending time with your family and me seeing mine?"

His frown became more prevalent at my words. "Well, it's not for the whole summer, we'll still have time to see our families. I was kinda hoping maybe after France you would come back home with me to meet my mother, then we could go to Scotland to see Sam and your family."

I smiled. He wanted to spend the whole summer together, and while that sounded wonderful, that was a lot of traveling, and how would Mum and Dad take it? I frowned, but before I could say anything, Allen continued. "Look, you don't have to decide right this second. I can always get a refund on the tickets and we can do our own thing. I just wanted to do something nice for us, that's all, just like our time in London and Scotland over the last break."

His mention of our last holiday put a smile on my face. Those days together were some of the happiest I'd ever had and now he was trying to recreate that on a whole new adventure. I hugged him. "I'll call Mum and Dad and see what they think and I'll let you know if they're okay with it."

Allen hugged me back so tightly I thought he was going to break me in half. With that, we headed out to meet Alessia and Mark for dinner so the four of us could all catch up. Things were starting to feel like old times when we first all met.

Chapter 33
END OF TERM

The last few weeks of the term went by so quickly that it was hard for me to believe that this week was finals and then I would have to choose between going home for summer and spending the holiday with Mum and Dad, or going to the south of France with Allen then coming back to the States to meet his mum and maybe other family members. To be perfectly honest, I still wasn't sure what I was going to do. Everyone might think the choice was easy and I should of course go with him on the trip, and while I knew that was true, the bond between me and my parents made it hard as I wanted to spend as much time with them as I could.

Today was going to be a great day regardless. I only had one more assignment to do for the term and it was going to be my best one yet; all I had to do was turn in the paper I had written on a country in Europe. Being from Europe, I just wrote about home. There was no way I was going to fail. Then before Allen had his end-of-term performance, all of us were going out to a goodbye dinner, just like last time, as Alessia was heading home first thing in the morning and Mark was leaving a few days after. Plus everyone was going to want to know what I had decided to do, so I wasn't looking forward to that part as much as I was spending time with my friends. I finished getting ready for the day, made sure I had my term paper in my bag, and headed out the door to what was going to be a great day.

The campus was as busy as ever with not only the typical students running in all directions but families and parents had started coming into town to help with move-outs and graduation. The number of people was a little overwhelming for me and I could feel my anxiety starting to rise. I made my way quickly towards the building of my class to hand in my paper so I could get out of the amassing chaos as soon as possible.

When I made it to the building, I started to head up the stairs at the main entrance when I heard a voice from behind me. "Hey, David wait up."

I shuddered as I recognized whose voice it was and turned to see Anthony standing there. "Anthony, I can't do this song and dance right now, I need to get to class." I turned to continue heading up the stairs but before I could Anthony grabbed ahold of my arm and spun me back around.

"I know that you don't want to see me right now, but I need to talk to you." He let go of my arm and took a step back. "But if you really can't do me this kindness, then go."

I frowned. "All right, fine, what is it?" I felt so small for giving in but the least I could do was humor whatever nonsense he had to say this time.

I guessed he was enjoying my pain as he had an enormous smile on his face. "I know I haven't made things easy and I know that I hid you when we were together, but I've changed now. I promise you, David, I've changed. Look, I'm standing here in this crowded place where everyone walking by can hear us telling you that I am in love with you and that I know I can make you happier than Allen ever will if you just gave me the chance."

There was a long pause. I didn't know what I could say that would not end up hurting him, and I wasn't sure how he would react and that scared me even more. Thankfully he continued, "Look, don't answer me now, think about it and let me know what you decide by the end of tonight."

I could not let this go on any longer or let him think that I would consider it. I went to speak. "Anthony, look—" But before I could finish my sentence, Anthony came up the stairs, grabbed me, and kissed me right there in front of everyone. I was shocked, but after a second I collected myself and pulled away. I was now in a full-on panic. I didn't know what else to do so I just said, "I have to get to class." Then I turned on my heel and ran as fast as I could into the building.

After I had turned my paper in and made it back to my apartment, I could not stop thinking about Anthony and what had happened. Why was I thinking about it, and why was I considering that I might have made a mistake by not giving him another chance? I always thought Allen was the one I wanted to be with, so why was I thinking that wasn't right either? I was so confused. I decided I needed advice from someone I knew would be honest, so I called Mum.

The phone rang and rang. I was starting to think she wasn't going to answer when I heard her sweet voice. "David, sweetie, how are you? Is everything okay?"

I smiled and felt much better just hearing the sound of her voice. "I'm good, I just needed some advice about love and boys."

Although I couldn't see Mum's face, I could tell she was smiling from ear to ear and was happy that I trusted her enough to call about a problem like this. "Of course, dear. So what's going on with you and Allen?"

I frowned and started to think maybe this was a bad idea, but decided to continue with my issue anyway. "It's not Allen directly. I've been confused lately. While I care for Allen and don't want anything to come between us, Anthony has been trying to express his love for me lately and I'm starting to think maybe I made a mistake not trying to make it work and giving up so fast and that I should maybe give him a chance."

There was a long pause before Mum started to talk. "Well, honey, I wish I could tell you what the correct choice is, but the only one who can know that is you. But if you care for these guys you need to decide to what capacity, and also take into account everything that has happened this last year. Whatever you choose, Dad and I support you. Also, have you given any thought to your summer holiday?" As usual Mum was right, I had to figure this out on my own. We chatted some more and I let her know that I hadn't decided on summer yet; I was planning to make my decision once I figured out this Anthony and Allen issue. After some more chatting, we said our goodbyes so I could get ready for my evening plans.

After I finished getting ready for dinner, I headed down to the lobby to wait for everyone else so we could walk to the restaurant together. Michael was already sitting down on one of the couches, and I sat down next to him while we waited for everyone else. Moments later the elevator opened and out came Alessia and Mark. We stood to greet them and we all started talking about our days while we waited on Allen. About fifteen minutes later Allen entered the lobby all dressed in his tux for his concert later with his violin in hand.

The five of us headed out the door and down the street. The night was warm and the sky was clear, making for a nice night out. We made it to the restaurant, sat down at the table, and ordered. The restaurant was nicer than most of the places we would usually go to, with white table linens, servers in vests and bowties, and menus on tablets. Everyone was talking about their plans and having a good time when the attention was then put on me. Michael looked right at me. "So, David, what are your plans for the summer?"

Such a simple question that should have such a simple answer, and now my insides felt like they were trying to get out of my body. "Well, Allen has asked me to spend some time with him, and Mum and Dad have been hinting for me to come on holiday with them, so I'm not sure yet, but it's going to be busy either way."

Everyone was just sitting there processing what I had said. Alessia chimed in, "Wait, Allen asked you to spend time with him, and you're not sure that's what you wanna do? I'm confused by this." Her eyes were darting from me to Allen, trying to read if something was going on with us.

Thankfully Allen was quick to respond. "I sprung a surprise trip on him without making sure he was okay with it first. I didn't know his parents wanted to spend the holidays with him, so I told him it was okay and to let me know later." He grabbed my hand under the table to let me know that he was there for me and it was okay.

For the rest of dinner, there was no more attention on me and what my plans were. We talked about Alessia's trip with her parents and that Mark was planning to come to visit at the end of summer. Michael was taking summer courses but being from the area it was not a big deal to him. After we finished our food we paid the bill and headed out to Allen's concert.

The five of us made our way through the crowded street as we headed for the concert hall. Once we were there Allen stopped in his tracks and was just staring. I looked to see what had caught his attention. I could not believe my eyes. Anthony was standing by the door dressed like he was attending the concert. My mind was racing. I could only imagine what was going on in Allen's head, let alone the others when they noticed. Anthony saw us and started to walk over. Allen grabbed my hand and started to squeeze it tightly as a way to let me know he was not happy with this situation and wanted to get out of it as soon as possible.

When Anthony made it up to us, the whole group was looking at one another in confusion, wondering who had invited him. He smiled. "Hey guys, it's nice to see everyone. Look, I know I've been a class-A dick, but I miss you guys and was hoping I could join you tonight and we could be friends again."

Alessia smiled, and she and Mark said they would like that, then said they would go get seats and made it clear to Michael to come with them. After the three of them walked away, Allen went off with a rage. "What in the actual fuck are you doing here? What makes you think David or I would want anything to do with you after everything?"

Anthony flashed a wicked smile that made my heart drop. "Didn't you know David and I have been talking again? He wants me in his life, and if you're going to be in his you're gonna have to deal with that, now, aren't you, Allen."

Allen gave me a look like *are you serious right now?* "I can't deal with this, David. You need to handle this. I have to go in and get ready." Allen let go of my hand and walked off quickly into the building.

Anthony and I both just stood there looking at one another before he spoke up. "Well, that went well, don't you think?" He let out a loud laugh and I just smiled.

"What are you doing here, Anthony? For real, what are you trying to achieve with surprise appearances all over campus just to talk to me?"

His smile turned into a frown. "I'm serious, David. I want you in my life and I want to be with you, but if you can't see that I'm better for you than Allen, who just walked off on you by the way, then I'll do whatever it takes to be around you till you figure it out."

The awkwardness between us was getting too much for me. I don't know what came over me but I blurted out, "I haven't made my choice yet." I quickly regretted my words but it was too late, I had said them, and the smile on Anthony's face was as big as I had ever seen.

I shook it off the best I could, trying not to make a mountain out of it. We headed inside and found Alessia, Mark, and Michael. I tried to sit between Alessia and Michael, but Anthony made sure that we were right next to each other. I just let it go as I was not trying to cause a fight in the middle of the hall and make Allen more upset than he already was. The five of us tried to make small talk and eventually, the lights lowered and the series of endless concerts was underway.

While sitting there trying to listen to the various musicians play their pieces and the professor talks in between, my mind kept spinning. What was I going to do? Was I going to give Anthony another chance, and what would this mean for Allen and me if I did? Was I going to go to France with Allen? How would this affect Anthony? What about my third choice: should I go home to Scotland and go on holiday with Mum and Dad? It would give me a chance to get away from this drama, but only temporarily. I would still have to figure it out once back, and that could make things worse. I was so confused and mad that I was making this so hard for myself. Why was this so hard? It should be simple. I was with Allen, and Mum and Dad already said I should go on holiday with him, so what was holding me back?

I came out of my thoughts when I felt something brushing up against my hand. I looked down to see Anthony was rubbing the top of my hand with his finger. I knew I should pull away but I didn't; instead, I let him continue while listening to the professor talk. Allen was next and I was excited to hear him play. Allen came onto the stage, and after the applause had stopped he lifted his bow and started to play. The song this time was "A Thousand Years." As he played I could feel his pain and emotion in every note. I loved it when Allen put his whole soul into his music. At this moment Anthony had gone from just rubbing the top of my hand to now holding it. I squeezed back for a moment before I pulled away. I was so confused. Did I still have stronger feelings for Anthony than I was letting myself think, and had Allen's song made me realize this? But at the same time, I knew Allen played that specifically for me. He always played songs based on what was happening with us. My mind was in a whirlwind. Allen finished and we all applauded. Once we stopped and Allen had walked off the stage, my mind was starting to clear, and I could finally think straight. I knew what my choice was now for the summer, and I knew which one of these two guys I was truly in love with.

To be continued.

Don't miss out!

Visit the website below and you can sign up to receive emails whenever C. S. MacInnes publishes a new book. There's no charge and no obligation.

https://books2read.com/r/B-A-NPGHB-XLUZC

BOOKS 2 READ

Connecting independent readers to independent writers.

Milton Keynes UK
Ingram Content Group UK Ltd.
UKHW041849311024
450516UK00002B/2